"You've got to pr... remove the blindfold."

"Okay."

Quinn had no problem with her demand. In fact, he was beginning to realize that not knowing anything about the woman he was involved with lent a definite edge of excitement to their encounters.

He could put up with his burning curiosity about her real identity in exchange for more moments like this one. The precise click of her heels approaching across his marble floor had his naked body tensing in anticipation. And he wondered what she'd do first. Touch him? Kiss him?

She walked behind him, the scent of her light perfume teasing him. He ached to reach out and tug her into his arms, dip his head into her mass of hair and inhale a lungful of her heady fragrance. But sensing she wished him to remain compliant, Quinn stayed still.

For now.

Blaze™

Dear Reader,

Every woman has probably fantasized about a man who was unattainable, a man she didn't dare go after. Most of us never get beyond the fantasy stage. But as a writer, I get to live vicariously through my characters and make those fantasies a reality.

Maggie Miller is a woman who dares to risk everything for love—at least, one night of it. And to entice practical Maggie to do the unthinkable, I had to summon an irresistible man, a man with the creative genius of movie mogul Quinn Scott. A charming, powerful, wealthy man with one wish—for a woman to want him for himself, alone.

I love the title of this story. *Bordering on Obsession* manages to capture the blinding need felt by Maggie and Quinn, characters who dream big and pit themselves against tremendous odds. If you enjoy this book, please watch for Kimberly's story, *A Burning Obsession*, available next June.

Happy reading,

Susan Kearney

Books by Susan Kearney

HARLEQUIN BLAZE
25—ENSLAVED
50—DOUBLE THE THRILL

HARLEQUIN INTRIGUE
682—ROYAL TARGET
686—ROYAL RANSOM
690—ROYAL PURSUIT
705—DADDY TO THE RESCUE
709—DEFENDING THE HEIRESS
713—SAVING THE GIRL NEXT DOOR

BORDERING ON OBSESSION

Susan Kearney

HARLEQUIN®

TORONTO • NEW YORK • LONDON
AMSTERDAM • PARIS • SYDNEY • HAMBURG
STOCKHOLM • ATHENS • TOKYO • MILAN • MADRID
PRAGUE • WARSAW • BUDAPEST • AUCKLAND

To Brenda Chin.

ISBN 0-373-79100-3

BORDERING ON OBSESSION

Copyright © 2003 by Susan Hope Kearney.

This edition published by arrangement with Harlequin Books S.A.

® and TM are trademarks of the publisher. Trademarks indicated with ® are registered in the United States Patent and Trademark Office, the Canadian Trade Marks Office and in other countries.

Visit us at www.eHarlequin.com

Printed in U.S.A.

1

"'YOU'RE OBSESSED WITH ME,'" he said, looking up from the script in his hand.

Yes, I am. More than you know.

But Maggie Miller suppressed the thought, and instead dutifully recited her line. "'And you can read my mind.'" She kept her eyes lowered to the bound pages on her desk so that her boss, legendary movie writer-director producer Quinn Scott, wouldn't read more in her expression than she wanted him to see.

Like the fact that she found Quinn's mouth more tempting than a hot fudge sundae with whipped cream and a lush cherry on top. Like the fact that her heart battered her ribs like a sledgehammer. Or that if she hadn't been sitting behind her desk, her legs might not have supported her.

It was all Quinn's fault for providing a show she couldn't ignore. In his excitement over the script, he may have forgotten he'd been on the way to his shower, but she hadn't. His sweatpants hung low on his hips and, bare from the waist up, his shoulders and chest glistened with moisture. His angular frame made her mouth water as he strode into the office after his daily workout. A script in his hand, a white towel around his neck and yards of bronzed skin beckoning, he could have been half Greek statue and half movie star.

Totally yummy. And off-limits. Maggie Miller wasn't some newbie secretary enamored by just any man. Oh, no. She'd been working herself up into a lusty lather over her oh-so-handsome, oh-so-sexy boss for a good four years now. Playing the good administrative assistant, she'd tried to keep her tongue from hanging out of her mouth, but, damn it, when Quinn asked her to read hot lines from his latest script, the fantasy seemed too real.

It was bad enough that Maggie dreamed of him all night and woke up with thoughts of him every morning, but reading love lines back to him bordered on insanity. Especially when Quinn didn't have the slightest idea of Maggie's feelings.

Unfortunately for her, Quinn regularly dated voluptuous blondes, international beauty queens and Hollywood's leading ladies—not the efficient secretary he'd inherited from the man he'd replaced.

Maggie drummed her fingers on her desk. Quinn would never suspect her feelings because he never even really looked at her. How could he when she hid the real Maggie behind her businesslike clothes? To keep her position as Quinn's oh-so-capable assistant, Maggie had buried her real self. Well, she was done watching Quinn go from one lucky woman to another.

Quinn's cell phone rang before he could read his next line. He checked caller ID, and tossed his script onto Maggie's desk. "We'll finish reading the scene later. I need to take this call.'' Then he disappeared into his office.

Maggie stacked the scripts on top of a towering pile and sighed. Doing something, anything, to get over her uncontrollable preoccupation with the man had become not only necessary, but absolutely imperative. However, since her goal of becoming a casting agent might very well depend on Quinn's goodwill, she didn't want to risk their working relationship by making a move in his direction.

And after this morning's phone call, Maggie had the chance to lure her boss into bed. Maggie had answered the phone to hear Laine Lamonde's harried agent explain, ''Laine's jet had engine trouble. She's landed safely in London, but I'm afraid she won't cross the Atlantic in time for her date with Mr. Scott.''

Of course the French film star wouldn't be caught dead traveling on a commercial airline. And since Laine was stuck in London, Maggie had the opportunity to take the actress's place—if she dared to seize the moment.

Maggie wanted much more than to arrange Quinn's day—now she intended to rearrange his night. She wanted her turn. Just one luscious night. A wild fling.

This time, instead of some vapid starlet, Quinn was going to escort the woman he depended on to keep his extraordinary life in perfect working order. If Maggie's plan succeeded, and her plans usually did, Quinn would never know his secretary had taken Laine's place for the evening's masquerade party. She would get her night of passion—and without risking the loss of her job, her future as a casting agent, or the friendly rapport she shared with her brilliant boss. With Laine's cancellation, Maggie had a doozy of an opportunity. And she intended to make the most of it.

"Knock. Knock."

Maggie looked up from her desk to see Kimberly Hayward, Quinn's protégé and Maggie's friend walking into her office, carrying spools of film under her right arm and the dress that she had picked up from Laine's hotel room in her left. Acting like a thief afraid of being caught, instead of Quinn's favorite production assistant, Kimberly glanced right, left, and back over her shoulder. She even checked Quinn's closed office door, before holding up the dress and whispering, "What do you think?"

Maggie had no trouble imagining herself dressed in the cerulean satin strapless gown with bead-encrusted bodice, and despite the butterflies swarming in her stomach, she grinned. "It's perfect."

Kimberly reached into her pocket and handed her an envelope with a receipt attached. "The concierge signed for these babies then sent them up to Laine's hotel room."

With her hand only trembling slightly, Maggie opened the envelope. A sapphire-and-diamond necklace with matching dangling earrings poured into her hand. "Nice."

"If you're still going through with your plan—"

"Of course I am." The image of wearing that dress for Quinn excited her almost as much as the idea of taking it off for him. She'd never been an exhibitionist, but now…her lust for Quinn was causing her nipples to harden and stand out enough that she wrapped a sweater around her shoulders and let the sleeves dangle down to conceal her arousal.

"You'll need this, too." From her leather bag that hung from a thin shoulder strap, Kimberly pulled out a mask that matched the gown and that would cover the wearer's face from eyebrow to upper lip.

A thrill of anticipation chased away most of Maggie's lingering doubts. Never mind that Quinn had never noticed her body. Never mind that in the last four years he'd never once so much as flirted with her. With the mask and the dress to hide Maggie's identity, she could be her real self. Slightly breathless at the boldness of her plan, Maggie stroked the blue feathers along the edges. "Thanks. I couldn't pull off my little deception without your help."

Kimberly had even taken the gown to wardrobe for a refit, and she'd requested a studio limo to take Maggie to her hairdresser and makeup artist before dropping her off at the hotel, where, disguised as Laine Lamonde, she would meet Quinn.

Kimberly set down the film and carefully hid the dress in a white garment bag, then hooked the hanger over the file cabinet handle. "You haven't changed your mind, have you?"

Maggie had a major case of the hots for her boss and she was tired of trying to ignore it. Such a silly infatuation had never happened to her before. She had no idea what the hell was wrong with her, but backing down was out of the question.

She was fed up with sharing a bed with her cats.

Tired of putting her personal life on hold for the sake of her career. Tonight opportunity beckoned. She had a chance to lure Quinn into bed.

But the slightest gesture or intonation could give her away and, despite her determination, she hesitated. "What if Quinn figures out who I am?"

"He won't. Don't worry. You'll have fun," Kimberly urged her on.

Easy for Kimberly to say. She wasn't the one taking the risk. Maggie was. Yet at age thirty-two, Maggie needed a change from leading her smart, sensible life, ruled by clothes that deemphasized her curves and a take-charge attitude that scared away most men. While she was hardly the mousy librarian type, she wasn't the kind of woman who swished into a morning meeting with Jennifer Aniston hair wearing a tight sweater and swinging a Prada handbag from a diamond-Rolexed wrist, either. In other words, she was a professional assistant valued for her efficiency and brains. Quinn would never consider her as a ready and available woman—not unless Maggie took drastic action.

Since she didn't do casual, no other man could be a substitute lover. No one else captivated her like Quinn could, but *he* didn't do serious. In the beginning, she hadn't even liked him—well not much. Of course, she loved his face—that was a given—and nobody wore a suit like Quinn. And while she admired the way he wheeled and dealed his way through Hollywood's A-list, she wanted some of his famous attention on her.

She sighed in frustration at her dilemma.

Trouble was, Maggie didn't want to transform her entire life. Going after Quinn as Maggie would put her beloved career in jeopardy as well as her future plan to open her own casting agency. But as Laine? No risk—except one of discovery, which she had covered.

Kimberly hitched her hip onto the corner of Maggie's desk. She was even more ambitious than Maggie. Kimberly wrote screenplays and wanted to direct and produce. Like Maggie, she'd been off men for a while, putting her career first and, while Maggie valued her advice, she knew all too well that Kimberly was living vicariously through her.

"What's the worst thing that could happen?" Kimberly prodded.

"If Quinn finds out what I'm doing, I could lose my job."

"You want to open your own casting agency anyway." Kimberly grinned. "Besides, he'll never suspect that his capable and practical secretary can show him such a good time."

Maggie tossed back her bangs and lifted an eyebrow. "I don't yet have the funds to open my own agency." Twice Maggie had been close to saving enough cash to start her own business. But then her sister Ronnie had had a difficult third pregnancy and been forced to stay in bed in the hospital. Maggie had flown home to Michigan and taken care of her niece and nephew so Ronnie's husband could work days and spend evenings with her sister. Although Maggie had lived for free at her sister's house and enjoyed the time with her family and niece and nephew, she'd still had to cover her apartment lease, car payment and insurance in California which had taken a drastic bite out of her savings. After she'd returned to work, she'd built up her bank account slowly, but then last year her mother had taken a terrible loss in the stock market, and Maggie had used her savings to help out her folks. As a result, she was no closer to starting her own casting agency now than when she'd come out to California after finishing business school ten years ago. So if Quinn found her out, he might not only fire her, but he was powerful enough to blackball the casting agency she dreamed of someday opening. Carrying through on her scheme would risk not just a steady paycheck but her future.

Maggie sighed, furious with herself for even hesitating. "Quinn isn't stupid. He picks those types of women for a reason, don't you think?"

"You aren't worrying that you aren't a glamour girl again, are you? I mean, I'm glad you're not. I'd have to hate you if you were."

With Quinn's films having won five Oscars including Best Picture, the famous writer-director-producer could have any woman he wanted. Competition for his attention was fierce. Aspiring actresses regularly accosted Quinn on the tennis court and during power lunches. Last week, Maggie had had to evict from his office a Playboy centerfold, wearing five-inch stiletto heels and nothing else.

"You can do glamour," Kimberly egged her on. "It's another side of you that every woman has."

Kimberly sounded so positive. Maggie wished she could be just as positive. "You're sure?"

"You just need the right man to let out your wild side."

"I suppose you're talking from personal experience here?" Maggie muttered. It was all fine and good for Kimberly to encourage her, but Kimberly wouldn't be the one taking the risk—or the one reaping the reward, she reminded herself. Finally she had the chance to touch Quinn's heat, to taste his mouth, to know what it felt like to have all that power inside her.

Kimberly blushed. "Hell, I haven't seen that side of myself, either, but I know that deep down under our practical natures are bombshells just waiting to emerge. And unlike you, who has found the right guy, I'm just waiting for a man to inspire that part of me."

"Quinn's not Mr. Right. He's Mr. Right Now." At thirty-two years of age Maggie ought to have better control over her hormones. She was way beyond the age of a teenage crush. Yet, here she was considering a scheme as risky as any that Quinn had ever dared and she only prayed her plans would turn out as well as his always did.

"How can you be so sure he's not Mr. Right?" Kimberly asked.

"I want to make sweaty, sensuous love to him, but my heart couldn't take more."

"Huh?"

"He's not the kind of man to commit to one woman."

"Maybe it's *your* issue."

"Come on. You work with him every day. The guy goes through women like other men go through socks.

A lady for every day of the week. Besides, I've been here under his nose for four years and he's never noticed me. If he only does so when I take off my clothes, that means it's lust and only lust—which is just fine for one night.''

"Okay."

"I'm not sure he's capable of falling in love. However, right now I'll settle for one fantastic dream night, so I can move on to the right kind of guy.'' Maggie frowned at Quinn's closed door, then narrowed her eyes in speculation at Kimberly. "And I'm not trying to be just any blond bombshell. I'll be impersonating Laine Lamonde.''

"You took six years of French. You do the accent well. And your features are even similar. That's why you can't let another chance go by.''

"Maybe so. But my hair's a dead giveaway. Hers is a lighter shade of blond and long.''

"You can add hair extensions, along with highlights this afternoon.'' Kimberly used her own kind of logic, encouraging Maggie to go after Quinn. Kimberly might not have oodles of experience in the men department but she understood Maggie needed one night with Quinn to get over this obsession. And Maggie in turn helped Kimberly with her career, not that she could do much besides periodically remind Quinn that he had her friend's screenplay on his desk and had yet to read it.

"I'll look different with the long hair and the dress,'' Maggie admitted. "But if anyone knows when a woman is acting, it'll be Quinn.''

"He won't be thinking clearly after you stir up his hormones."

Kimberly's imagination spurred Maggie to chuckle at the thought of leading Quinn on, teasing him, seducing him. While she wouldn't normally catch the eye of the ruggedly gorgeous, arrogant-as-hell Quinn, she would look just about perfect in that designer gown. Not far behind her intellect was her next best asset: her body. She worked out regularly, alternating between kickboxing and yoga, and the mask would hide her pretty, but not out-of-this-world-gorgeous face.

Between the dress, the limo and the jewelry, she just might convince him that she had star quality. Even a man who had been characterized by *Time* as a sensitive and creative genius could be fooled by the right woman with the right incentive.

Tonight, she could be that woman. Boy-oh-boy, she had the incentive. Just thinking about Quinn's magnificent body made her toes curl and heat seep between her thighs.

Even without her conversation with Kimberly, even without her need to find out if Quinn was as good as her obsession, Maggie couldn't seriously consider not going through with her plan. Quinn had too much raw sex appeal for her to resist, too much intensity in those eyes she wanted on her. This was her moment to grab, her time, and if she didn't, she'd regret the lack of courage for the rest of her life. Maggie would rather live with a mistake than a regret. She'd rather lament what she'd done than what she hadn't done. Besides, while she admired Quinn's intellect and creativity and appreciated how he wielded his power, Quinn was still far from infallible. And although he was rarely alone, she knew he was lonely—a trait that Maggie found almost as devastatingly irresistible as his bold brilliance.

But, mainly, Maggie was done denying her attraction to him. Last week, she'd celebrated her thirty-second birthday, and all those candles on the cake seemed to be telling her that if she didn't make a major change in her life, next year she'd again be out celebrating with the girls and then returning home once more to an empty bed.

And as if she'd needed more encouragement, the morning following her birthday party, she'd cleaned out her medicine chest and found that her unused tube of diaphragm jelly had expired a year ago. So she'd decided enough was enough—she had to do more than dream and hope and fantasize. She was stoking up her love life before it extinguished permanently from disuse.

Maggie considered other major turning points in her life. Losing her virginity to her high school sweetheart at seventeen. Moving to California after college. Meeting and becoming friends with Kimberly. She didn't regret one of those decisions. It was likely she wouldn't regret taking Quinn to bed.

She was going to take advantage of this opportunity.

She enjoyed her life and her friends, but she wanted more than working toward a goal of opening her own casting agency. She wanted romance. And while she'd had two long-term relationships, nothing interesting had occurred in the sex department for the past two years.

Still, taking her boss to bed was rather drastic, one of her more outrageous ideas.

"As long as Quinn doesn't object to my wearing the mask in bed I should be fine."

"Why should he mind?" Kimberly asked.

After months of sexual frustration, Maggie was up for a little kink in her sex life. She'd spent too many nights fantasizing about Quinn to back out now. But no matter how many times she told herself that Quinn was just as arrogant and egotistical as he was creative and charming, she couldn't talk herself out of her fascination with the guy.

She wanted to taste those lips. She wanted to feel his arms around her. She wanted his hands on her breasts. She'd tortured herself long enough. Of course she'd tried to shove him out of her dreams, but had failed miserably. She'd had enough of fantasizing. To get over him, she needed the real thing.

Sensing Maggie's decision to go through with the plan, Kimberly's eyes sparkled with vicarious pleasure and her tone teased. "Are you sure you're ready for hot, sweaty sex with Quinn?"

Oh, yeah. She was more than ready. Just thinking about him made intimate flesh thrum, and her blood simmer. Maggie carefully placed the jewelry on loan into her purse before answering Kimberly. "This scheme is insane, you know that?"

"Several mind-blowing orgasms are all you need to work him out of your system. Going on like you have been, *that's* insane. You want the guy. Go after him, girlfriend. Or you'll spend your old age regretting you let life pass you by.''

Maggie sighed, knowing Kimberly was right, teetering on the edge of going forward. ''Sex for the sake of an orgasm has never before been enough for me. Yet, Quinn doesn't do long-term relationships. So, this is solely for one night.''

Kimberly rolled her eyes at the ceiling. ''Since you know that fact going in, you won't even get your heart nicked. But why are you convinced that he's so wrong for you?''

Maggie stood from behind her desk and began pacing. ''He's a maverick. I'm pragmatic. He's a moviemaking genius. I'm just his assistant. He spends his nights with legendary movie stars and I practice abstinence—''

''Not anymore.''

''—and he's a lover boy.''

''You ever heard the saying that opposites attract?''

''He's twenty-eight. I'm thirty-two.''

''You're not yet ready for the old-age home.''

Maggie bit her bottom lip. ''I've told myself a hundred times that we don't fit together. It does no good.''

''Exactly.'' Kimberly beamed. ''The only way you're going to shake your infatuation is to have him naked in your bed for one night.''

''And what about after he treats me like all the other women in his life?''

''After a delicious one-night stand, you'll be over the guy.''

Kimberly was probably right. Hooking up with

Quinn would be Maggie's right of passage, would allow her to move on into the more mature and stable relationship that she really wanted. The logic was outrageous—and irresistible, just like Quinn himself.

Maggie's pacing ended at the office door, and she turned back to Kimberly. "Suppose he doesn't want to go to bed with me?"

"What man can resist Laine Lamonde? Besides Quinn needs to please Laine if he wants to sign her for his next project. Somehow I don't think he's going to have a problem with taking her to bed. She's the sexiest woman to come out of France since Catherine Deneuve."

"Exactly my point."

"Are you saying you can't do sexy?" Kimberly challenged her.

Knowing her eyes flashed with annoyance and sexual frustration, Maggie frowned. She felt wound up so tight, she shouldn't have any trouble at all acting the way she felt. Hot. Bothered. Sexy as hell. "I'm saying I'm taking a huge risk."

"Laine's never been to the United States. People here don't know her at all."

Maggie picked up the mask and placed it over her face. Immediately she felt bolder. Brazen. Kimberly was right. She'd stewed for long enough about the possibilities. It was time to act. She could do this. "Nothing ventured, nothing gained."

2

HOTEL VENDAZ PERCHED on the top of a cliff overlooking the Pacific Ocean, the lavish grounds a sparkling setting for hosting a masquerade party. The impressive staff greeted repeat customers by name. The waiters were familiar with their wealthy and famous guests' favorite foods. And the bartender had to be the most discreet in L.A.

The bar, polished and dark, where patrons could drink and sample complimentary hors d'oeuvres, did a brisk business, not much different than twenty years ago. The first time Quinn had come here with Jason, his famous father, Quinn's head hadn't reached the bar stool, yet the bartender had smiled kindly at him and handed him a ginger ale with three cherries. And he'd thought the place a marvel. He'd sensed the power in the men and sipped the aura of the deal with his soda.

As one of Hollywood's leading action stars, his father was known by everyone. Thanks to plastic surgery, a strict diet and three hours a day with his personal trainer, his father looked as good as ever and commanded upward of twenty million dollars a picture. Men and women alike fawned over Jason, as if he were as precious a commodity as a box-office hit.

The air of glamour had affected Jason's son. From an early age, Quinn appreciated the women who smelled like expensive perfume, liked watching the men's ritual of clipping cigar tips and enjoyed hearing the industry gossip before it made the next day's papers.

And he'd quickly learned that the real power in film wasn't in the stars or the writers or the directors, but in the money men who put the deals together. By age ten, Quinn had decided to follow in Steven Spielberg's footsteps. He wanted to do it all—write, direct and produce movies so he could control the project from beginning to end. From the conversations of his father's associates the business side of the film industry had seeped into Quinn's pores.

And Quinn had learned about life and love by watching his father's abundant affairs and his mother's four marriages and divorces, concluding that love was erratic and capricious. But the work, the creation of a movie, had always been the stable part of his parents' lives.

Jason Scott may have shown his son the power brokers behind the action, but it was Quinn's mother, a famous director, who taught him about angles and lenses long before Quinn had ever attended UCLA's prestigious film school. But even his mother accepted that the real deals were made on the golf courses, over linen dinner napkins in gourmet restaurants and in the Hotel Vendaz bar.

"Why are you drinking all by yourself?"

From his favorite seat at the end of the polished bar, Quinn looked down and frowned at Dan O'Donnel. At no more than five-foot two, Dan had to crane his neck to look him in the eye. He wore a cowboy hat, jeans, boots and a flannel shirt, his costume for the party.

Quinn nodded a short greeting over his bourbon. "I'm waiting for someone."

"Aren't we all." Dan slid onto the stool beside him, his feet dangling. He accepted a beer from the bartender and raised his glass.

Short in stature, but long on guts, Dan had come up through the ranks, first writing, then directing and now producing—which might have been admirable if he weren't Quinn's foremost competitor in obtaining funds to green-light his movies. While the men had a social relationship, Quinn wouldn't qualify it as friendly, partly because Dan's personality grated on his nerves. Right now the two men who were employed by Simitar Studios were competing for the ear of Derek Parker, the CEO. But Quinn felt he had the edge. He knew Derek Parker had a thing about Laine Lamonde. If Quinn could sign her to his next project, he would practically assure himself of the funds needed to green-light his picture. However, a rival like Dan could never be discounted and Quinn remained wary. Dan had a reputation for stepping on toes and for a mind like a steel trap. But as they shared the same profession, they also shared similar problems.

A big problem was heading their way, making a beeline for the bar. Lynn Parker, a C-grade actress, currently married to Derek Parker, thought she should be cast as a leading lady in someone's, *anyone's*, film. Although her looks were good enough, put the woman in front of a camera and she had as much animation as a dead fish. Handling Lynn's ambition was always tricky since, one wrong move, and Derek could refuse to fund any of Quinn's many projects. While Quinn had aimed high and succeeded in his goal to emulate Spielberg in the writing, directing and producing of movies, he had yet to go out and start his own studio. Therefore, he must avoid offending Lynn Parker at all costs, but at least she wasn't one of those women who pretended to be fascinated with Quinn on a personal level when she wanted a part. Lynn was more straightforward.

Lynn placed a kiss on Quinn's cheek. "Found me a great part, yet?"

"Not one good enough to showcase your talents."

Behind Lynn's back, Dan rolled his eyes. He regained a stoic look as she turned and stooped to kiss him, too. "What about you? I've heard the part in *Lady Luck* might be right for me."

"Sorry, you're much too young."

Lynn bought the lie, preened and walked away, pleased by Dan's compliment.

Aspiring and established actors and actresses regularly accosted producers for jobs. So did writers, directors, musicians and people in advertising. Quinn rarely met anyone who wasn't trying to sell him something or who didn't want a favor, like finding work for a family member or friend. While he enjoyed his work, and his power and his stature in the industry, the limelight had drawbacks—such as having to turn down unqualified people. Someday, somewhere, he'd like to find a woman who wanted to be with him strictly for himself, not what he could do for her career.

"I don't know how much longer I can keep making up flattering excuses," Dan muttered into his beer.

"You might not have to for much longer," Quinn replied. "She's taken a fancy to the pool boy."

"When Derek finds out, he won't be pleased."

Derek Parker kept his pretty wife as a cover for his long-term male lover, a closely guarded secret. Actors might get away with dabbling in alternative sex lives, but the money men were conservative. It was okay to have a mistress young enough to be their granddaughter, but a long-term love affair with a same-sex partner was frowned upon. And with Derek's power to green-light a film, neither producer said a word to the other about the latest gossip that Derek and his lover were quarreling.

Since Quinn and Dan were currently going head-to-head for funding at Simitar Studios and Derek's backing was necessary, talking in a crowded bar where their conversation could be overheard would have been foolish. However, Quinn's thoughts didn't stay on Derek or Dan but wandered to the lovely Laine Lamonde. With luck, tonight he'd sign Laine and solve his problem. Quinn hoped Laine's English was good enough to have a conversation. However, he'd once signed a French actress who couldn't speak a word—some things didn't need a translation.

Like tonight's date, most of his evenings spent with actresses were for publicity or to conduct business. If Quinn had cared to disabuse people of the notion, and he didn't, his dates usually ended after a little business, some picture taking for the magazines and sound bites for the publicity department. Then he and the woman would go their separate ways.

He expected this evening to follow the same path. And then, the writer, director and cast, along with the all important financing would fall into place.

Dan peered over his beer at Quinn. "Where's your costume?"

Quinn pointed to a black mask in his pocket, a cape tied over his shoulders and his sword leaning against the bar. "Don't you recognize Zorro when you see him?"

"I don't recognize anyone in these damn masks. It makes working the room…difficult."

"Then I suggest you just enjoy yourself tonight. That's what I plan to do."

"I heard you have a hot date with Laine Lamonde." Dan cocked his brow. "If you're planning on signing her as your next leading lady, you might think again."

"Really?" By not so much as a blink of an eyelash did Quinn reveal his surprise and irritation that Dan knew of his plans. But he still damned the Hollywood grapevine that was faster than the Internet. Of course, if he signed Laine, the press would work in his favor. And if not… He didn't consider failure. She would sign because the part was perfect for her talent.

Recovering without changing expression, Quinn let the minor annoyance of his competition knowing his business slide off his shoulders. By the end of the evening, most of the people there would have recognized Laine and the speculation would start. Were the French star and the producer sleeping together? Getting married? Having a baby? If they left together, the paparazzi would have their pictures in their weekly rag under some ridiculous headline.

"Laine's a real pain in the ass," Dan told him with a devilish grin. "On her last shoot, she demanded that all the cameramen wear black shirts, black slacks and shoes, even black socks. She didn't want their clothing to distract her." Dan's eyes narrowed as he took in Quinn's black tie and shirt that matched his black tuxedo and mask. "But then you already knew that, didn't you?"

"I'll keep your warning in mind." Quinn didn't reveal that he'd already heard the rumors, didn't want to admit that he'd chosen his attire with the lady's preferences in mind. After all, he fully intended to give Laine whatever she wanted—as long as she agreed to his terms.

Quinn's beeper went off, signaling to him that the studio's limo carrying Laine had arrived. He finished his bourbon and left a healthy tip.

"Duty calls." Quinn picked up his sword and went to meet the lady, his mask still dangling from his fingers.

Laine Lamonde was a sensation all over Europe and could go nowhere without being mobbed by legions of fans. More important, she oozed sex appeal and had a face that could convince consumers to buy perfume, diamonds and Jaguars. Quinn suspected Derek Parker's instincts for another blockbuster hit were right on target this time. Although Quinn and Laine had never met in person, he'd studied her face, a face that made love to a camera lens with effortless ease. And she had a sexy voice that he'd never heard speak English, but the sound of her French put a jaunt in his step.

Quinn wanted to watch her grand entrance. So much could be learned from the way a woman walked into a room. Some danced, others skipped, some dragged their heels or staggered from partying too hard before they arrived.

After exiting the bar, Quinn strode across the marble floor of the hotel lobby. Celebrities flowed back and forth from the ballroom to the lobby and socialized in groups large and small among huge potted flower arrangements. More business deals happened at these kinds of fund-raisers than back in the offices, and he spent most evenings in places like this or at parties in Beverly Hills.

"Quinn, darling." Hanna Owens, one of television's greatest writing talents had bumped into him. "I have a script—"

"Hanna, I'm always pleased to look at anything you write. Have your agent messenger it over."

"It'll be on your desk tomorrow morning."

Quinn's request to peruse her work was sincere. And one of his greatest pleasures was buying work from writers he genuinely liked. All too often after agreeing to read someone's efforts, Quinn had to pass on their project. That's why he still hadn't read his production assistant Kimberly's screenplay. It was one thing to reject a stranger's work, another to have to reject the work of someone who worked for him, someone he liked and respected as much as he did Kimberly.

Several actresses tried to stop Quinn. While he nodded hello, he kept moving.

"Hey, Quinn." Max Weinberg shook his hand. A critic for *Film Tomorrow Magazine,* the reviewer had panned Quinn's last film, *Sugar Honey,* calling it a beastly mix of arrogant art and nonstorytelling. Then *Sugar Honey* had won an Oscar. Sometimes this business could be sweet.

"Max."

"I hope you didn't take my review personally."

"I take everything about my films personally," Quinn countered and moved on into the crowd. His comment had been calculated to draw attention and it had. As he walked on, he could hear a pleasant buzz of speculation behind him. Buzz was always good. Let them think he had the world by the tail—because in this business, impression was everything.

"Quinn," Carly Kenner reached up and straightened a collar that didn't require smoothing. But as one of his mother's oldest and dearest friends, she was entitled to a piece of him. "Is Stella going to direct your next film?"

He shook his head. "Mom won't finish the African film in time."

"Well then, dear, please keep Michael in mind. He's very creative, you know."

Michael was Carly's son. He had lots of talent, but he never brought a film in on budget.

Quinn squeezed Carly's hand. "It's not always up

to me. The stars these days have their favorite directors.''

''I'll count on you to do what you can.''

''All right.''

Two directors and an advertising executive tried to corner Quinn behind the potted gardenias. Again, he spoke briefly and continued to shoulder his way through the crowd. A half dozen people stopped him before he reached the entrance, but he'd anticipated and planned for these minor delays.

Finally he donned his mask.

As usual, his timing was impeccable. In the blue Versace gown that the studio had supplied, Laine Lamonde was a sight he wouldn't have missed. Even with the mask that covered her face, he couldn't take his eyes off her and neither could anyone else. Her breasts filled the bodice of the strapless dress, and the tight waist added more dimension to her curves. She wore a large sapphire-and-diamond necklace that nestled between her breasts, but it was neither the dress nor the sparkles that drew attention.

Laine had star quality. That indefinable something that said *Look at me. I'm bold. I'm confident. I'm beautiful. I'm a S-T-A-R.*

Quinn was impressed—if she was trying to create gossip for her American debut, she was succeeding with a capital *S*. He found himself holding his breath even as he took in her effect on the crowd. Almost everyone in the room was A-list, so to make any kind of impression was a challenge. But Laine was special, exuding charisma in spades.

Photographer's bulbs flashed. Microphones were

crammed in her face, but she didn't pause. The French actress didn't walk, she floated across the floor in an elegant display that turned heads in a room where heads didn't turn easily. She was magnificent, a sight to make the mouth water.

With a saucy grin, Laine strode straight into Quinn's arms and kissed his cheek. She hadn't played games, pretending she didn't recognize him, which upped his estimation of her a notch.

"Quinn." She spoke his name with only a slight French accent. "So good to meet you."

Her perfume was light, sensual. Her greeting warm, yet dazzling. Quinn couldn't remember the last time a woman had intrigued him. Perhaps it was the lady's mask. Or the reputation that preceded her. Either way, she possessed that star presence that couldn't be defined, had that certain something that made people look at her and keep looking.

It wasn't the flawless skin or the dress or the million-dollar jewels. It was her personality that oozed through. Sexy. Saucy. Seductive.

"I've been looking forward to our evening together," he told her. Her eyes were more blue in person than on film, but perhaps that was due to the lighting or her mask. And although she was naturally stacked, her hips were slimmer than he recalled.

No matter. Actresses changed their bodies with exercise and diet and surgery as often as they changed their hair color.

"Is what they say about you true?" she asked as she tucked her arm through his.

"What do they say?" he asked curiously.

"That you're *un amoureux fantastique.*"

"Excuse me?" He didn't speak French but had caught the word *amoureaux,* lover. Women often propositioned him during a first encounter, but they were mainly starlets, looking for a fast way to a part. Laine's agent should have told her that Quinn was ready to offer her the lead.

"I flew all the way over from France for you."

She must not understand the impression she was giving him. Her English couldn't be translating well. Quinn chose his words with care. "I'd like us to work together."

"*Non. Non.* No." She waved her arms in a grand gesture of impatience.

She spoke a long sentence in French and he only picked up one word. *L'amour.* Maybe she was saying that she loved his work. But her tone was low and sexy. She sounded as if she was propositioning him. Maybe she did want to make love. But why?

Her reactions confused him. She certainly wasn't what he'd been expecting but maybe he was just reading her wrong. Since they'd just met, Laine couldn't have feelings for him, could she?

Yet she didn't seem to understand that he was ready to offer her the starring role. Going to bed with him wasn't necessary. Not that he ever did business that way. Quinn prided himself on his reputation for picking the best actress for the part on the basis of ability, not on whether or not he had a personal relationship with her.

So Laine had no reason to try to begin a relationship with him. He couldn't see what she hoped to gain and that not only confused him, but puzzled and intrigued him. What did she want? A rewrite of the script to make her part bigger? A role for a lover? A larger fee? Or was he simply suspicious when there was no reason to be?

Apparently the language barrier was going to be more difficult than he'd anticipated. "I'm sorry. I'm not sure that I understand."

"I did not come here for work. I came to play. *Oui?*"

"Play?"

"*Absolument.* To play...in bed. With you."

3

OH, THIS WAS FUN. Quinn wouldn't be this casual if he suspected that she wasn't Laine Lamonde. And since Maggie had fooled Quinn completely she wasn't anywhere near as nervous as she'd expected. Which had allowed her to act more boldly than she'd planned, throwing her arms around his neck and kissing his cheek.

Her blood poured through her veins like hot brandy. She might come from ordinary stock—her mother was an investment banker and her father a truck driver—but her parents had always encouraged her to go after what she wanted. Right now, she wanted Quinn.

He gazed down at her with amusement in his eyes. "You think I'm a play toy?"

She reached up and tugged his tie. "You're even wrapped up with a pretty bow."

Teasing a man who looked so handsome, sexy and mysterious in a black mask and cape, black shirt and black tie was even easier than she'd foreseen. She couldn't just blame his clothes, though they did emphasize the stunning looks he'd inherited from his movie-star father. With those piercing green eyes peering at her through the Zorro mask and those high-cut cheekbones framing his kiss-me mouth, she could barely stop herself from insisting he immediately accompany her up to her room.

"I'm glad you approve of my attire—" Quinn's eyes raked her gown "—as much as I approve of yours."

Maggie's shimmering blue gown lent her courage. The silk hugged her figure into an hourglass shape. The expensive necklace plunged suggestively between her breasts, the cool metal reminding her that if she played her role correctly, very soon Quinn's fingers would be skimming her sensitive flesh.

She let her fingers dip between her breasts to touch the bauble. "Please thank the studio for the loan."

Just as she'd intended, his gaze followed her fingers, then lifted to meet her eyes. He clearly knew exactly what she was doing, but he didn't seem to mind. In fact, he seemed pleased.

"The jewel couldn't have a finer setting," he spoke gallantly, with a touch of deviltry in his tone.

The mask allowed her to keep her composure and leap the gap from a yearning, ordinary secretary to a glamorous movie star. With her face hidden, she could use a provocative French accent, concentrate on walking with fluid grace, slightly exaggerating the sway of her hips. Piece of cake.

With her disguise a success, fears of losing her job and confronting Quinn faded. She could fit in with this crowd. She'd spoken to the big agents from CAA and William Morris often, and was on a first-name basis with many stars from her work in Quinn's office. She knew these people, their work, their interests and all the gossip. Maggie's practical side receded, allowing the glamour girl to come out. Full force.

The intrepid conversation came naturally as well. Why shouldn't it since she'd been practicing all day?

She had to give Quinn credit. At her announcement to make love with him, he'd subtly changed the subject. As if she'd made a *faux pas*. Except that his green eyes had dilated in interest. Although he hadn't directly responded, she'd surprised him, intrigued him. He'd steered the conversation into flirtation, but Maggie didn't have the time for a long roundabout flirtation. She only had tonight.

"*Monsieur*, I want us to be together. To make love."

Quinn raised a dark eyebrow, his firm mouth quirked up in amusement and interest. "You flew across the Atlantic to…take me to bed?"

"*Oui.*"

Quinn played the gallant gentleman to the hilt. Although he spoke in a voice low and thrumming with husky intensity, he truly didn't appear ready to take advantage of her. Perhaps he thought Laine's French wasn't translating correctly.

He tried again. "You realize that sleeping with me is not necessary for starring in my next film?"

Cute. And much too businesslike. She knew him well enough to know that he wanted her, but that he wouldn't allow his own passion to ruin a deal. For him, the deal was the be-all and end-all of life. He seemingly believed she thought that she had to make love with him to win the part. Foolish man—yet it was so endearing that he wouldn't take advantage.

Frustrating, too, though, because she definitely wanted him to take advantage of her.

"I said nothing about sleeping," she teased. "I can sleep in France."

"Your agent has explained—"

"I did not come here to talk business. That is a matter for you and my agent." She took his hand and placed it on her waist as she tugged him into the ballroom. Music from a live band set her feet swaying and her heart knocking. The feel of his fingers through the thin silk made her want to skip across the dance floor and turn cartwheels in her high-heeled shoes. "Dance with me, Quinn. Show me American romance."

Quinn did as she asked, smoothly taking her into his arms and sweeping her into the crowd of celebrities, high-powered agents, writers and directors. She recognized almost everyone, but her mind wasn't on anyone but Quinn. She even set aside the temptation to envision how she would cast the various stars once she opened her agency. As she'd just told Quinn, tonight was not about business.

A full head taller than most of the men, he had the dark machismo of a Pierce Brosnan or Antonio Banderas, the high-voltage grin of a *GQ* model and the presence of a tycoon. Lost in the music, with Quinn's body pressed to hers, she gazed into his dark green eyes to gauge his thoughts.

Uh-oh. She glimpsed his rising tide of suspicion. Maybe her accent had slipped for a second. Maybe, she was an inch too tall or short. Or maybe she wasn't acting the way he'd thought Laine would. Whatever the reason, she had to distract him quickly—before that perceptive mind of his caught on a snag.

Maggie didn't want him thinking. She wanted him feeling and reacting. To her. In one bold move, she reached behind his head, threaded her fingers into his thick, black hair and pulled his mouth down to hers.

He didn't hesitate—not even for an instant. For her, the crowd and music receded. There was only Quinn and her, standing chest to chest, hip to hip, thigh to thigh. The kiss might have been Maggie's idea, but that didn't stop Quinn from taking control. His mouth came down on her lips, his tongue delving, entwining with hers. There was nothing tentative in his kiss. He was all man, exploring and taking and demanding whatever she wanted to give.

And Maggie gave everything she had. She might not have kissed a man in over a year, but her lips made up for the lack of practice with enthusiasm. Since Quinn in the flesh was much better than Quinn in her nightly fantasy fest, she leaned into his hard masculinity, enjoying the scent of his suit, the aroma of his aftershave, the complete smell of him—all musky and male and yummy.

The temperature of the room was cool, but Quinn heated her from the inside out. His kiss was commanding, demanding and sure, yet tender at the same time. For a moment she felt as though he wanted her as much as she wanted him. Because the air around them crackled with their electric chemistry.

And when he finally broke the kiss and masterfully danced her deeper into the Hollywood crowd, he never glanced once from her eyes. It was as if he yearned to see behind her mask, behind her face, to discern what she really wanted. Almost as if he couldn't believe that she yearned to make love to him for no other reason than she found him incredibly attractive.

When the music stopped, her heart was beating a cadence against her ribs. Slightly breathless, she looked up at him, the heat in his eyes causing her toes to curl. "How long must we stay?"

"As long as you like." In the dim lights of the dance floor, she couldn't read his face. But his tone was guarded, as if he was thinking again. She needed to keep him off balance with passion but the dance floor was not the right place to make her move.

"Let's go somewhere more private, *mon cher*."

His eyes narrowed at her suggestion, as if he suspected a trick but was too polite to say so. "We just got here."

"Don't you want us to be alone?" She skimmed her hand over his silk shirt, pleased to feel the strength of his heart beat. She dipped a finger between two buttons and let the pad of her fingertip graze his bare flesh. She'd dreamed of this moment so many times, but her dreams fell short of the reality of being so close to Quinn. Of finally doing exactly what she wanted. His skin was smooth, muscular and dusted with a light covering of hair. The clothes that she'd admired earlier now seemed a barrier.

"We could retreat to the bar," he suggested. "To talk."

She cocked her head. "Talk is not what I have in mind."

"Hmm."

"I do not want to delay my pleasure. Or yours." She laced her fingers through his, enjoying how his large hand warmed hers.

He brought her hand to his lips and kissed her knuckle. "And how do you know there will be pleasure?"

"A woman knows."

"What else do you know?" he asked, his tone polite, but deep with desire. As they left the ballroom together, many heads turned to watch them go.

She didn't care about the gossip and gently squeezed Quinn's hand. "I was right to come here. We will be very good together."

Quinn tilted his head to one side, as if thinking hard again. "Odd how we barely know one another, yet I feel as if we've known one another for—"

"After tonight, we will know one another much better, *oui?*" She couldn't let him go where he'd been going. She didn't want him thinking that he knew her better than the stranger she was supposed to be.

She used her free hand in a wide sweeping gesture and steered him toward the elevator. "Tonight doesn't have to be complicated. As you Americans say, I want you. You want me. What could be more simple?"

As they rode the elevator up to the hotel's penthouse suite that the studio had reserved for Laine, Maggie leaned into Quinn, her arms wrapped around his neck, her mouth less than an inch from his. So far, her plan was working and the thrill of anticipation exaggerated her accent. "I am so happy you invited me here tonight."

They stood face-to-face, and he touched her mouth with his fingertip. "Such a beautiful mouth. And you speak English so well. If I'd known, I would have invited you over to do a film much sooner."

She yanked back from his arms and allowed irritation to enter her voice. "If you speak of business again, Monsieur Scott, I shall fly back to Paris."

His head jerked back at her outburst as if she'd startled him, but he recovered quickly. "I'm sorry. It's habit."

His apology seemed sincere and, since she believed him, she stepped close again, ran her hand along his close-shaven jaw and demanded, "A habit you will break for me?"

"Yes."

His voice, strong and sure, should have convinced her that he had no doubts at all about her, except Maggie knew Quinn so well that she caught a flicker of reservation in his eyes. The elevator dinged as they reached her floor.

She took his hand and led him through the double-leaded etched-glass panels, across the slick marble floor, past the elegant living room and into the luxurious bedroom suite that Kimberly had prepared earlier according to Maggie's directions. Silver tapered candles lit their path to the gold-and-emerald bedroom where she'd surrounded the king-size canopy bed with more candles. On the dresser, a bottle of champagne rested in a silver ice bucket beside two crystal flutes. The bed had already been turned down, the crisp clean sheets and fluffy down pillows waited in invitation.

She'd left open the sweeping floor-to-ceiling doors that overlooked the ocean to let in the clean scent of tangy sea air. Light jazz played over the stereo system and merged with the soft music of a waterfall in the gardens below.

Quinn paid no attention to the decor, his focus remained on her. He removed his mask, set down his sword and took her by the arm. "I don't know whether to be flattered that you went to so much trouble, or insulted that you think I'm so predictable."

She didn't like the questioning lilt of his tone, and decided subtlety had no place here. If she spoke, he could argue, and she didn't want to waste a moment.

She spun on her heel, giving him her back, and lifted her long golden hair. "Help me with my zipper."

If he'd been reluctant before, she had apparently changed his mind. He nibbled her neck. "I am accustomed to calling the shots."

"I am very determined."

"I admire that in a woman." He nipped her ear. "You also have a very beautiful neck. I admire that, too."

She'd never thought acting so brazen and uninhibited could bring her so much joy. Between wearing her mask and Quinn having no idea of her true identity, she had a freedom to say and do whatever bold thought struck her.

Time to go for broke. She lowered her voice to a

seductive whisper. "Unzip me and you might find other things about me that you like."

His fingertips brushed her nape, shooting a tingle of anticipation down her spine. His warm breath fanned her ear, and she had to stiffen her knees to prevent a tremble.

"You don't mind if I take my time, do you?" At his query, her mouth turned dry, but his question was clearly rhetorical. She was so ready for Quinn's touch, and yet, contradictorily, she wanted him to linger, so she could savor every precious moment.

And as he'd so casually reminded her, he was a man accustomed to calling the shots. So she remained silent, and he chuckled, his rich tone signifying a promise to edge her right over her comfort zone to another level where she'd never been. He tugged down the zipper several inches. The bodice of her gown parted in back and the front dipped from her flesh, allowing cool air to waft over her naked breasts.

"It may take me a while to explore all of you. I'm very thorough," he promised, his voice a silky caress. His fingertips stroked tiny circles on her neck and bared shoulders, parting the dress at her spine, edging the material aside. She stood for him, holding up her hair, the action raising her breasts which ached for the caress of his clever hands.

He was going too slowly. Now that he'd started the zipper, she could finish what he'd begun. She reached behind her back, tugged. And the gown pooled at her feet, leaving her exposed—except for her mask, a scrap of lace panties and her heels.

Quinn didn't miss a beat. "You have a marvelous back."

"*Ah, mon cher,* and what do you think of the front of me?" She turned around then, pleased at his intake of breath.

"You are a work of art—"

"Who wants to be touched." She placed her hands on her hips.

He reached…for her mask. His move took her unawares and she stifled a gasp. She'd thought he would go for her breasts. But no, Quinn had to be Quinn—unpredictable. He had to do the unexpected and think outside the box. But she'd planned as well as she could for this eventuality. If he didn't allow her to keep the mask, she would leave. But after all her elaborate scheming she was not yet ready to flee—not when the passion she craved was so close to fruition.

She stepped back, almost tripped in her haste. "It's your turn to take something off," she told him, forcing a playful tone into her French accent.

He loosened his tie. Tossed it onto a chair.

"More," she demanded.

He slipped out of his jacket and took a step toward her. She shook her head. "I'm practically naked."

"Mmm."

"And you still have too many clothes covering you."

With a wry lift of his lips, he reached for his belt and her mouth went dry. Quinn might call the shots at the office but not here.

"First, the shirt, *si'l vous plait.*" It was a powerful feeling to give him orders to do exactly what she wished. As he obeyed, unbuttoning his shirt and removing it in quick, efficient moves that left her breathless, her breasts ached and her nipples hardened into nubs so tight that she had to refrain from throwing herself against him.

She'd never seen his bare chest without a towel draped around his neck. And his powerful shoulders and sculpted abdominals revealed that Quinn liked to lift weights. But he didn't have the bulk of a wrestler, more the lean lines of a swimmer.

Maggie let her gaze sweep over him in appreciation. The candlelight reflected off his toned body, emphasizing the clean lines of his limbs, his tapered torso. The triangle of hair that spread from nipple to nipple and narrowed into the waistband of his slacks made her long to see more.

She licked her lips. "Now, the belt."

His eyes flashed with green fire. "You haven't removed anything in quite some time."

"I'm way ahead of you, Monsieur Scott."

He removed his belt. "An interesting way of telling me to strip."

"Now, your shoes. The right one first," she added remembering to act like a spoiled movie star. However, keeping up her role was becoming more difficult with every item of clothing that he discarded. No man had the right to be so beautiful. And that he was alone with her, stripping to her command, incited her with lust.

As if understanding her need to order him, he straightened without taking off his socks. His gaze zoomed in on her breasts and the heat of his gaze alone caused her nipples to tighten further. She trembled at the heat that simmered between her thighs.

Speaking past her quiver of need was almost beyond her. But not quite. She licked her bottom lip again. "Your socks."

On her command, he bent to take them off, revealing the powerful muscles of his back. Needing to restrain her galloping heart, she dropped her gaze to someplace safe. His feet.

But damn him. The man even had elegant feet. High arches. Long, straight toes, the nails neatly clipped.

Quinn straightened in one fluid move. He wore boxers, tented from his erection. She liked seeing his visible display of desire. Liked knowing that her little game had turned him on. Liked knowing that she could get under his skin.

And she was far from done.

"Would you like to remove my panties?" she purred.

"Yes." He closed the distance between them so quickly, she gulped.

Although he had yet to touch her, heat radiated from his muscular body. She summoned up another command. "Take them off. With your teeth, *si'l vous plait.*"

He stood so close, she saw his nostrils flare. "First, another kiss." He didn't wait for her to agree. His mouth swooped back down on her lips, and as her lips parted in invitation, he nibbled and nipped as if she were a morsel of chocolate to savor.

He took his time with her mouth, his inventive kiss

demanding and persuading. And yet, never once did their bodies touch, which naturally made her wonder just *when* he intended to get around to touching her, or removing her panties, or adjourning to the bed.

After years of waiting, she was about to get what she wanted. She was actually pulling this off. And Quinn was better than her dreams. Every bone in her body was melting from just his lips on hers, his tongue entwined with hers.

Quinn exhibited remarkable patience. She was ready to tackle him onto the mattress, and yet she sensed that although he was ready to make love, he wasn't quite as ready as she. She reminded herself that she'd had a head start, had devoted many nights to the fantasy of lusting after him, spent months of fantasizing about him, which had built her anticipation to explosive heights.

She broke their kiss. "My panties," she reminded him.

He placed his palms over her breasts and caressed her with smooth circling motions. "First, I want to explore the treasures you've already revealed."

She should step back. Retake control of their game. But his hands felt so good, she couldn't summon the willpower. And, damn him, he knew it. Somehow, he'd read it in her eyes, in the way she yielded to the temptation of his magical hands, his palms slowly circling, his fingers barely grazing her breasts. *My, oh my.* The sensations had her biting her lip to avoid moaning.

She didn't know how much more of this she could take. Then he added another level of seduction. His sexy voice. "You have perfect breasts. So soft and full and responsive. When a woman responds so eagerly, she makes a man feel like the greatest lover in the world. But you know that, don't you?"

I do now. "Yes." To her own ears, her tone sounded wanton. She couldn't be sure she was keeping up enough French words or the accent, couldn't be sure she wouldn't give herself away. But how could she concentrate when all she could think about were his hands on her breasts, his flat palms continuously caressing?

She placed her hands on his shoulders to steady herself, her fingers digging into his firm flesh. His skin was warm and smooth over his hard muscles. Heat over steel.

In comparison, her insides felt like a pool of water that threatened to break through its dam at any moment. She couldn't wait much longer.

"My panties…"

He dropped to his knees, but his hands never left her breasts, his stroking never ceased. And then his breath ruffled the goose bumps on her hips. His lips grazed her skin, and she realized she'd made a huge mistake. She might be calling the shots, but Quinn controlled the pacing. She should never have asked him to use his teeth. This sweet torture was going on far too long.

"Hurry."

"You sound as if you are begging."

She was. Damn him for knowing. Damn him for pointing it out. "You are the one on your knees, *mon cher.*"

"So I am." He chuckled and his breath tickled her, right through the lace. "And I'm exactly where I want to be."

His hands on her breasts were creating a direct and steady current to the heat between her legs. "I said to hurry."

He lightly pinched her nipples. She gasped in surprise and pleasure.

"Patience." He muttered with a muffled chuckle. Finally he had the panties moving down, but just an inch, before he turned his attention to her other hip. She closed her eyes in frustrated impatience, but as if sensing she was trying to protect herself from the sensations, his fingers again tweaked her nipples.

"Quinn. This is so very good."

"No." He placed his nose between the lacy scrap and breathed in. "This is."

He was right between her legs. He'd pulled down her panties only an inch, teasing her. His wondrous hands never stopped moving over her breasts, holding her in limbo, then flicking her nipples until she writhed in need.

She'd never been so ready for a man, so wet, willing and wanting. From the moment she'd stepped out of her dress, she'd been ready to go. And he'd made her wait when all she wanted was to feel him inside her. She forced her legs to hold her upright, if only for a moment more.

He licked her right through the panties, his surprise move shooting a sizzle of current in her most sensitive place. She forgot to hold back a moan. One lick. That was all he gave, just a taste. She wanted to spread her legs. But then he was back to tugging down the panties again, perhaps another half inch. And if she widened her stance, he'd never get them off.

"I'm waiting," he prodded.

"For?" She didn't want to talk. She only wanted to feel his wonderful hands and his erotic mouth. Not even in her secret fantasy fests had she allowed her imagination to go this far, hadn't known she could experience this level of hedonism without gratification.

"I'm waiting for you to explain." He sounded so patient. She was ready to scream. "Explain?" Was he on to her? Did he know she wasn't Laine?

She couldn't allow him to stop now. She'd say anything. Do anything. If only to keep his hands and mouth right where they were.

He licked her again. "Tell me the real reason why I'm here with you."

4

PANIC MERGED WITH SEXUAL frustration. Did Quinn suspect? Did he know she was Maggie? How could she keep a rational thought in her head when he kept licking her between questions? When his hands kept tweaking her sensitive nipples? When she had to fight to keep back the tiny moans of pleasure threatening to escape her throat?

Maggie didn't have an answer for him. Neither did Laine.

He licked her again, shooting fire through her panties. With the rough lace and his hot tongue on her, she couldn't think.

And when she heard thunder, she thought the roaring came from the blood rushing in her head. But when she turned her head, she saw the answer to her problem and seized it. "It's going to storm."

Quinn paid no attention, his tongue and hands busy. She wanted to shout for him to take off her damn panties. To remove his boxers. To sheathe himself inside her. Here. Now.

But Quinn was on his own time schedule. And he knew just how to bring her to the brink, then back off while she panted and gnashed her teeth.

Lightning flashed in the distance. Storm clouds

rolled in over the sea, blowing in gusts of cool air, extinguishing some of the candles. "Quinn, I need…to…close—"

Oh, Lord. The things he could do with his tongue.

Wind brought in the first tiny droplets, just a mist, but a forerunner of what was to come. The cool vapor on her heated skin gave her the impetus to step back from his hands and magical tongue. "Quinn, it's going to rain."

He reached for her. "So?"

She slipped away. "So, we should shut the door."

He stood and frowned at her, a trace of doubt in the jut of his jaw. "You're worried about the carpet?"

Uh-oh.

Laine wouldn't have concerned herself about the wet drapes and carpet. But Maggie lived in a world where people had to worry about the consequences of their actions. And habit, combined with sweet sexual torture, had made her forget her role.

She had to distract him fast. She hooked her thumbs into her panties, cocked her hip, shot him a saucy grin, then she spun around. Slowly, oh-so-slowly, she peeled the panties down over her butt—thanks to hours of kickboxing—her nice tight butt. When she glimpsed him over her shoulder, his eyes had the fierce look of a man who only by the power of supreme control held himself in check, and all the hours in the gym were worth her effort.

His voice went hoarse. "You're exquisite."

"Oui," she agreed, pleased he was pleased. Even better she'd distracted him again. And given herself

a few moments to regroup. Pushing him out of his zone of control excited her more than she'd imagined.

She bent over farther as she tugged the panties past her thighs. He sucked in a breath, then let it out with a slow rasp that made her burn. She bent forward a little more as she guided the lace over her knees.

Curious that he seemed to be holding his breath, she glanced between her legs, found him staring at her with utter fascination and spiking lust. His expression—a mixture of awe, adoration and shock—made her flush with heat.

However, the mask kept Maggie from the slightest feeling of embarrassment. She'd made love before, but never like this. Never had she done anything so wild. Never had she felt so free. Or so hot.

When she stepped out of the panties, she deliberately widened her stance. And Quinn, like a tiger sprung from a trap, pounced as she straightened, grabbing her up into his arms.

He held her with one arm behind her knees, the other behind her back. Her heart pitter-pattered at the romantic gesture—but there was nothing romantic about the fierce look of tension on his face.

She thought he'd carry her to the bed, but he strode past the bed, through the bedroom and headed out onto the balcony where lush potted plants preserved their privacy, even from any boats at sea.

''The door,'' he ordered, his face dark with ferocity.

She removed her hands from around his neck and pulled shut the sliding glass door behind them. The major part of the storm was far out to sea, but the fringes whipped wind at them, rained on them, perfectly matching the wild glint in Quinn's eyes.

He no longer looked like the boss she knew. His pupils reflected the lightning in the distance and his heart thudded against her cheek. Tension radiated from his arms and those proud shoulders held her like a pirate about to ravish his lady.

Maggie wanted to purr. She'd stirred up his passion, liberated the savage, and she couldn't wait to reap the rewards of her efforts.

When Quinn set her down at the balcony's edge, he gripped the railing, one arm on either side of her, trapping her. Even if she wanted to change her mind, there could be no retreat. With her little striptease act, the gallant side of Quinn had snapped, releasing the elemental Quinn that made her breath catch in her throat and the heat between her thighs flare another degree.

She reached for the waistband of his boxers and yanked them down. "You still aren't keeping up, Quinn."

He held up a silver foil packet between two fingers as if the condom were a prize. "I had other things on my mind."

She ignored the condom. As if attracted by a magnet, her fingers closed around his sex. Long and thick, he felt hard, slick velvet to her touch, and he leaped at her caress. Perhaps because she lightly raked his skin with her nails, perhaps because she used her fingers to cup his balls, he strained at each caress.

She blew out a sultry breath of air. "I like having you in the palm of my hand."

"I'll just bet you do." The hard edge of his voice warned her that she was playing with fire, that only his forbearance and immense control allowed him to hold completely still for her. "I just hope...you're ready...for the consequences."

Beneath the mask, she licked her bottom lip, thrilled by the broken cadence of his utterance. "Thanks to your tongue, I'm more than ready. However, I thought I should return the favor."

His fingers clenched the sleek railing. Raindrops slicked down his heated flesh. And at her tantalizing suggestion, his erection swelled even larger, his skin stretched tighter. She flicked her thumb over the engorged head and was pleased to hear him groan above the rush of the wind.

"I'm going to find all your sensitive places with my fingers, then again with my tongue," she told him, enjoying his struggle to hold completely still for her caresses. "I'm going to take you so close to orgasm that you can taste release."

"Promises. Promises," he egged her on.

She spoke in her French accent, softly, seductively, with the strength of a woman who intended to incite uncontrollable lust. His. And hers. "And just as you think release is at hand, I'll deny what you want most. Can you agree to that, Quinn?" she challenged.

"Bring it on."

His pupils dilated until his eyes looked black. His mouth twisted with the pleasure and pain of waiting to see how and where she would stroke him next. And she took her time, lingering when he writhed. Marveling at the strength he used to let her do as she wished.

She'd never before had her heart thunder with this kind of feminine power. Holding him in her hands, drawing his body so taut that his muscles clenched, learning his feel and his scent gave her a boost of conviction that she wasn't tempting fate, but fulfilling her destiny.

Tonight, at the height of the storm, with the lightning in the distance and the clouds raining down, she and Quinn were fated to be here. Together.

With the waves pummeling the rocky beach below in her ears, urging her to do more, she kneeled and took Quinn into her mouth. He tasted of wind and rain and pure male heat. And just as she'd promised, she took him to the brink.

And pulled away, to watch the wildfire in his eyes transform to a slow burn. Water spiked his lashes and trickled down his chiseled cheeks, accentuating the raging appetite consuming him and engulfing her.

He loosened his grip on the rail and grasped her shoulders. "Tell me what you want," he demanded.

"You."

With his teeth, he tore open the condom. "You're going to have me, darling."

She snatched the packet from his mouth and kissed him while she unrolled the condom over his straining sex. She took the opportunity to tease him again, to heat him up just another notch. But at the same time, his hands were all over her, sliding, stroking, seducing. Their mouths fused with a conflagration that should have melted them.

He shocked her by breaking their kiss and whipping her around to face the storm-tossed sea. From behind her, he placed her fingers on the balcony, demanding in her ear, "Keep your eyes open."

"Why?"

He parted her legs, eased them away from the railing, leaving her open and waiting for him, almost in the same position as when she'd teased him earlier by removing her panties. Water lashed her back, pooled, trickled between her legs.

But he didn't give her time to think. "Watch the storm as I take you."

She quivered, ready for him to enter her. She should not have been surprised that he chose to exhibit more finesse and draw out the pleasure. His hands dipped between her thighs, and in her high heels, her bottom was tipped up at just the right angle for him to place one finger inside her. One very erotic finger that stroked and caressed her G-spot until a new kind of pressure built.

She needed him to touch her clit. Just one stroke would shoot her tumbling over the edge.

But, of course, he made her wait. And squirm. And she watched the sea toss and churn, her breasts quivering, her mouth hungry, her body helpless to do more than take everything in, feel the need building to new heights, praying that she wouldn't be reduced to begging.

"Quinn?"

"Yes."

"I want you inside me, damn it."

"I know."

And he kept right on stroking her, ignoring her demand, until she gasped for air. "You don't…know."

"Sure I do," he teased with words and with his fingers. "You told me, remember?"

"I take it back."

He chuckled. "Too late."

"But—".

"I'm going to take you to the edge until you can taste it." He tossed her own words back at her.

Her legs trembled, communicating her need, spreading her desire until her entire body trembled, clenched with the fire he so carefully stoked. Despite his words, just one more caress and she would explode.

And he stopped.

He stood, pressed his chest against her back, his sex jerking urgently against her, his hot breath rasping in her ear. She bucked her hips to take him inside, but he reached for her breasts and tweaked her nipples, shooting electric heat to her core.

He bit her ear. "Wait. Wait. Wait."

"But—"

"Watch the storm."

She'd been so busy with the storm inside, she'd forgotten to watch the thunderclouds scudding across the sky. Lifting her face to the rain, she observed the distant lightning. And Quinn nuzzled her neck, nibbled her shoulder and stroked her breasts. He tugged on her nipples, playing with the hard tight buds between thumb and forefinger. She writhed in need.

Gulped back a scream.

And finally, when he plunged into her, she was so

hot, so slick that she climaxed in a wild tempest. She would have collapsed if his strong arms hadn't held her.

Her galloping heart eventually slowed, and she realized that he was still inside her, still hard. He dropped one hand between her thighs and began to play with her sensitive clit all over again.

Oh my. Oh my. She'd thought she had no more to give. She'd thought she'd released every degree of passion she'd been storing up for Quinn. But she was wrong.

From the embers of the inferno he'd created inside her, he rekindled the blaze. With his lips buried in her neck, his hand on her breast, his cock deep inside her heat, he was over her, around her, inside her. She was wrapped in Quinn. And nothing had ever felt so amazingly good.

And this time when she exploded, shattered into a zillion tiny bundles of bliss, she shouted his name. Took him with her to new heights.

She'd gone for broke to be here with him, and she'd succeeded beyond her wildest fantasies. Quinn had created the passion she'd craved, given her a night to keep her warm during the coldest winter. No matter what happened next, Maggie would never forget their time together. Quinn had filled these hours with the sweetest and most passionate lovemaking she'd ever experienced.

A while later, as she slowly returned to sanity, she noted that the torrential downpour had abated to a sprinkle, and Quinn's rasping breaths had ebbed to a steady rhythm. He held her close while the cooling rain washed over them in a cleansing downpour. She didn't want to move, just wanted to remain with him, the contentment filling her completely.

But, of course, as much as she would have liked to spend the entire night with him, she couldn't—not without the risk of him learning her real identity.

QUINN WOKE UP TO THE SOUND of his cell phone. Immediately wide-awake, his brain kicked into high gear. First, he noted that he was still at the hotel. Second, that he was alone. And third, that according to the time on his cell phone, he'd overslept. Caller ID told him that his father was on the line. Quinn held the phone up to his ear. "Hi, Dad."

"You're late. Was she pretty?"

Most fathers, most stars, would have been annoyed that their son had obviously slept in and forgotten their breakfast meeting. But not Jason Scott. Not the movie star who went through women faster than plastic surgeons used up silicone.

"Very pretty," Quinn answered.

"Anyone I know?" At the question, Quinn winced. He didn't want to think about the possibility that his father might know Laine in the biblical sense. Although this was her first time in the States, his father's films had often been set in Europe. He and Laine would know the same people, attend the same parties.

Quinn sighed and looked for a note on the pillow. Nothing—not a scrap of paper. Still suspicious of Laine's motivations for making love with him last night, he realized he was surprised that she'd disappeared this morning without asking him for anything.

Quinn ran a hand through his hair and restrained a sigh of frustration. "I can't keep up with your women, Dad."

"You sound as disapproving as your mother."

"Sorry." Quinn winced. While he wasn't the playboy his father was, he would be hypocritical to pass judgment on anyone after last night. Laine and he had practically set the bed on fire. On the other end of the line, his father remained silent, waiting for Quinn's explanation. "She was real special, and I hope you *don't* know her."

Jason chuckled. "What's her name?"

"Laine Lamonde."

"You're in Paris?" his father asked.

Quinn rubbed his forehead. "I'm at the Vendaz."

"With Laine Lamonde?"

It wasn't like his father to question him so thoroughly. Quinn strode into the bathroom, looking for a note on the mirror. A clue that they would meet later and she'd finally tell him what she wanted from him. No note. Nothing. "She's not here at the moment. Why?"

"Well, the morning news said Laine's jet had engine trouble, but that she set down safely in Paris last night."

"Dad, you know those rags are pure gossip. You can't believe a word you read."

"Whatever. My agent just walked in. Catch you later."

Quinn wasn't accustomed to spending the night with a woman and waking up alone—without any explanation. Odd. There was no note. No phone message. No Laine there to greet him with a kiss and whatever the hell she wanted.

Last night might have been the most erotic encounter of his life, but the incredible sex hadn't completely veiled his earlier suspicions. Laine had been sexy as hell. She possessed that incredible star quality, and yet she hadn't wanted to talk about her role, her leading man, or the script as he'd expected. If she hadn't bowled him over with her sexuality, he might have been more suspicious, asked more questions. But the moment she'd come on to him, he'd known what he'd wanted—her.

Now, all his senses went on full alert. He could still smell her scent, but as he collected his clothes, he noted that hers were gone. He ducked into the bathroom. No personal items sat on the counter. No toothbrush. No cosmetics. Not even a hairbrush.

He stalked back into the bedroom and opened the closet. Empty.

The dresser drawers. Also empty.

No note. Not a shoe or a stocking or a hairpin. And Laine had vanished without asking him for one damn thing.

It didn't add up.

Quinn slipped back into his clothes with a smile. If she wanted to playact the mysterious lover to catch his attention, her scheme was definitely working. Laine had surprised him from the moment they'd met and she'd kept surprising him all night. Now again this morning with her disappearing act. The woman definitely had a flair for drama. However, now she really had upped his suspicions. What was the minx up to?

No doubt he would find out soon enough.

Quinn drove home, showered and changed before heading to the office, his body satiated from last night's lovemaking. And the entire time he couldn't get Laine out of his mind.

Images of her standing there in her heels and panties and mask as she'd ordered him to strip. A vision of her bending over to remove those panties. A snapshot of her standing on the balcony in the storm, demanding that he enter her.

If she could create half the heat on film that she had in the bedroom, they'd have a blockbuster on their hands and the lady might win an Academy Award. She'd been a fantastic lover. A seductive woman. A mysterious tease.

He couldn't wait to see her again. Mostly, he had let her call the shots and had enjoyed seeing her use her feminine powers to turn on the heat. And, oh, did she know how to ignite the fire. Although he'd had every intention of winning her agreement to sign a contract, he was far from disappointed. She'd thoroughly convinced him that her English was good enough, the French accent light enough, to wow American audiences. More important, mixing business and pleasure hadn't been a mistake. There could be no doubt that she'd enjoyed herself as much as he had.

While he looked forward to their next meeting, he still couldn't keep his suspicions at bay. Why had she come on to him last night? Women frequently offered to make love with him, but they usually wanted something in return—and he ended up bothered that he wasn't wanted for himself. Not for the writer-director-producer Quinn but for Quinn Scott, the man. Laine's refusal to discuss business had intrigued him from the start, and after lovemaking when she still hadn't mentioned a thing, he'd assumed her demands would come in the morning. But then she'd up and left before he'd awakened, and now he found her game even more fascinating.

While the film would be shot in Vancouver, the city was just a short hop in the company jet, so Quinn could see her again. He wasn't sure what exactly about her had so intrigued him, but she'd stolen his full attention and kept it from the moment they'd met. Exotic, erotic, she was a fascinating woman.

But first Quinn would phone her agent, make the contract arrangements and perhaps take her to dinner tonight to celebrate.

He parked his car and then strode into his office, pleased with himself and his plans. It wasn't every day that Quinn so looked forward to working with a new star. It was even rarer that he got so stirred up over a new woman in his life.

Maggie handed him a fistful of messages and a cup of coffee. "Morning." She didn't comment that he was late and he liked that about her.

"Morning. Anything important?"

"They're all important."

He sipped the coffee, waited for a jolt of caffeine to hit him while he looked at her. As usual, Maggie had her hair up and wisps fluttered around her face.

She had a stack of contracts on her left, bills on her right and in front of her was a computer screen that showed a log of every phone call into the office.

"Tell me."

"Your dad—"

"Already talked to him."

"Three agents. One director. Peter Rege—"

"Who?"

She didn't miss a beat. "The writer of the film being shot at Malibu," she reminded him, "has called every fifteen minutes for the past hour. He *says* it's an emergency."

He could tell by her dry tone that she didn't believe there was any emergency. He depended on Maggie to screen his calls and to remind him of his meetings, but he also respected her judgment. "What's up?"

Maggie grinned. "The director won't let Poopsy on the set, and Rege can't think up new dialogue without her."

Quinn lifted an eyebrow. "Poopsy?"

"Rege's pet poodle."

"Ah."

"Apparently Poopsy keeps barking at the leading lady, so the director barred the dog. Now Rege claims he can't write any new dialogue."

"Take care of it, please."

Maggie made a note. "When Rege calls again, I'll tell him that you're thinking about hiring a new screenwriter."

Maggie was the best assistant Quinn had ever had. She knew how he thought, and he trusted her to make decisions in his absence. Sometimes he thought she could do his job as well as he could.

"What else?"

"Have you read the script Kimberly dropped on your desk?" Maggie could also nag. They both knew he hadn't read the script. And he hadn't missed the fact that she and Kimberly had become good friends. Which really made him avoid reading the script. Chances were it was good, but not fantastic, and Quinn only worked on the very best projects. Every idea had to be meticulously researched, authenticated and tested. And he didn't want to have to tell Maggie or Kimberly that her work wasn't up to his exacting standards. He didn't want to hurt her or discourage her. So he avoided reading it. However, even he knew he couldn't put off both women forever. Maggie was too loyal to Kimberly to let him forget, and Kimberly was too determined to succeed not to keep reminding him, too. Quinn realized he was surrounded by bossy women. Maggie and Kimberly, and now Laine.

Quinn shook his head, and Maggie pointed her pen to the stack of messages. "You should answer those."

"Okay."

"Any message from Laine?" he asked.

"Should there be?" Maggie, a bit flustered, glanced at her computer screen to check the log. "No. Nothing. Her agent called yesterday. That message is in your hand."

Quinn nodded and sauntered into his office. He shut the door, then thumbed through the yellow slips.

There. Maggie's neat handwriting. He read aloud. "Laine's plane delayed in Paris."

His stomach tightened. But Laine must have taken a commercial flight. Quinn sat in his chair behind his desk and pressed the intercom that connected to Maggie. "Get me Laine's agent on the line."

A few minutes later, Maggie buzzed Quinn back. "Tyrol's holding for you. Line three."

"Thanks, Maggie." Quinn pressed the button. "Tyrol. Sorry I didn't get back with you yesterday."

"No problem. Laine's mechanical problems are fixed, and she told me last night that she should arrive in New York today. She wants to do some shopping and then head out to the coast early next week. We can do lunch."

Next week? Lunch?

Quinn almost dropped the phone. His thoughts raced. If Laine had spent last night in Paris, then she couldn't have been with him.

He hadn't made love to Laine Lamonde last night.

Rarely surprised, never mind stunned, Quinn functioned on automatic pilot, but sweat broke out on his scalp and the fine hairs on his neck stood on end. "Fine. I'll have Maggie set us up for lunch."

Meanwhile, his thoughts repeated, helplessly confused. The woman he'd made love to last night *hadn't* been Laine Lamonde. That's why the woman had refused to take off the mask. He'd thought she just wanted the mask to heighten their sexual encounter. No wonder she hadn't spoken about the business. That's why she hadn't asked him for anything.

Damn. He'd been played for a fool. But why? Had

his mystery woman been an actress trying to go after Laine's part? Did she think that by seducing Quinn he'd cast her as the lead in his next picture?

Damn it to hell. Quinn didn't use a casting couch. He chose the best actress for the part. And he tried like hell to keep his business life separate from his private life. However, with a face as well-known as his, people recognized him. Used him for their own designs.

He'd been in the business way too long to consider the possibility that some woman had just wanted him for himself. After watching his parents, he doubted he'd ever been that naive.

So who had he made love with last night? And what had been her motivation?

Even as his anger spiked and receded, he couldn't keep his curiosity from burning. He damn well wouldn't give the woman a part in his film. However, crazy as it seemed he wanted to see her again. They'd been that good together.

But how could he find her again if he didn't know her name?

5

KIMBERLY SAUNTERED TOWARD Maggie's desk, reels of film under her arm again. She was the most underused, talented gofer in Quinn's employ, but she showed up with a friendly grin. "So how did the big date go?"

"Shh." Maggie glanced at Quinn's closed door.

"You pulled it off? He doesn't know, huh?" Kimberly set down the dailies, reels of film that she picked up at the airport and delivered to Quinn's office every morning.

Maggie kept her voice to a low murmur. "Quinn just spoke to Laine's agent. He must have just learned that the woman he made love to last night was not the French movie star."

"From that Cheshire grin on your face, I'm assuming he still doesn't know that you took Laine's place?"

"He doesn't have a clue." And though Maggie hadn't so much as closed her eyes last night, she was still revved on adrenaline. She'd made love to Quinn and kept her real identity secret. She'd fooled her boss completely. And she'd had a great time and still had her job to boot. Her plan had come off without a hitch and she felt as if she was floating on air.

This morning, before sunrise, she'd sneaked out of the hotel, and after returning to her apartment, she'd used the hair color her hairdresser had given her to restore her hair to its normal color. She hadn't bothered with the hair extenders. With her hair pulled up onto her head, no one could see the length.

"Well, you look pleased and sated."

"Mmm."

"So on a scale of one to ten, how was he?"

"Off the chart."

Kimberly helped herself to a cup of coffee. "You going to share some details, or do I have to beat them out of you?"

Maggie grinned. "Be nice, or I won't nag him into reading your script."

"Oh, please. I need some vicarious fun."

"Use your imagination," Maggie teased. "Better yet, find yourself a hunk and take him to bed."

"Fine. Keep the good stuff all to yourself. I'll just march into his office and ask Quinn about his evening."

Maggie knew Kimberly would do no such thing. She was still too in awe of Quinn's reputation, something she'd have to get over if she wanted to make it in the business. But most important was that Kimberly would never betray her friend. There was a deep sense of honor that came through every word she wrote.

Calling Kimberly's bluff, Maggie shooed her toward Quinn's door. "Go on. Maybe he'll think *you* were his mystery date."

"Like he'd believe that for a New York minute."

Kimberly glanced down at her chest. "I don't exactly have the right-size equipment."

Quinn picked that moment to barge out of his office. Kimberly jumped and spilled her coffee all over her shirt. As she mopped it up and mumbled about cleaning up in the rest room, she made a hasty departure, leaving Maggie to face her boss alone.

Oh, God. Maggie had made love to her boss and he didn't know it. If he ever found out, she'd want to die on the spot. While the sex had been terrific and she'd gotten more than she'd wanted, the fling was done. Over. The man was so wrong for anything more than what they'd already shared. Quinn didn't do long-term relationships—not with anyone. With parents like his, he probably wasn't even capable of making any kind of commitment. So why was excitement zinging through her veins?

Maggie took one look at his tight lips and realized this was not the same charming and debonair man-about-town as he'd been the night before. This Quinn was annoyed, on edge.

Good. He had it all too easy with women constantly chasing him. And she was happy to upset his equilibrium—even if he didn't realize she was the woman who had done so.

Maggie eyed him with feigned concern. "Something wrong?"

"Damn right." His eyes narrowed. "I want another private line put in my office by tomorrow. Run the new phone number in the classified section. No, take out a full-page ad." She had to refrain from grinning at the outrageous gesture he was planning. "Make sure I'm billed personally—not the studio."

"A full page?" She'd underestimated his degree of upset and a tingle of sheer satisfaction shot through her. She supposed that enjoying his suffering was mean. But after years of fantasizing over him while he ignored her, she could live with herself.

"And see how fast you can rent a few billboards."

Billboards? The idea was pure Quinn, outrageous, expensive, totally off-the-wall. Maggie schooled her face to reveal nothing and started writing on a legal pad. "You paying for this, too?"

Quinn scratched his brow. "Don't nag me with details."

"Far be it from me to nag."

"Good. I have enough woman trouble."

She couldn't resist teasing him a little more. "Woman trouble? Not you? Not one of *People* magazine's Ten Most Eligible Bachelors?"

Maggie bit the inside of her cheek to keep from grinning. Quinn rarely lost his temper. The man was too controlled, too on top of things to lose it. But as he paced in front of her desk, his long legs covering huge chucks of carpet, his shoulders ramrod straight and his eyes lit with an inner fire, she could see that he was worked up, all right.

"This is serious."

"Right. You want the ads and the billboard to have your new private phone number along with your name? Quinn Scott, movie producer? I hope you have nothing better to do than answer the phone because it's going to ring off the hook. Or have you forgotten that everyone wants to be a movie star?''

''Okay. I'll have to be discreet.''

Maggie held the pen poised over her pad. At least Quinn was so worked up that he didn't notice her amusement or her excitement at having taken such a risk. ''Buying a full-page ad and placing billboard advertisements across L.A. isn't exactly what I'd call discreet.''

Quinn stopped pacing long enough to glare at her. ''Then what would you suggest?''

''Me?'' Maggie scowled at him. ''I don't even know what we're talking about,'' she lied. But of course she did. He wanted to find the woman he'd made love to last night. He wanted to find *her*. She almost chuckled, but sucked it down and released a choking sound. Even telling herself he would be spending a small fortune for no reason didn't banish her amusement. As one of the wealthiest men in Hollywood, he wouldn't miss the money.

''You okay?'' Quinn asked, back to his pacing. She'd underestimated him a little. Despite his furious strides across the room and his bad mood, he'd still noticed she'd bit back that last chuckle.

To distract him, she went on the offense. ''You going to explain to me what's going on?''

''No.''

She tossed her pen onto the pad and leaned back. ''Okay.''

''Yes.''

She just stared at him, marveling at how quickly the man changed his mind.

"Okay." She didn't pick up the pen, just watched him pace. Quinn really had terrific energy. And stamina. Last night, he'd lasted for hours. And he'd been a wonderful lover. But now he was being incredibly stubborn. Once he got an idea in his head, he didn't let go of it. But he might change his mind a dozen times before he settled on a final strategy.

"I don't know."

As she'd predicted, he'd changed his mind again.

Maggie tried to insert equal parts sympathy, frustration and sarcasm into her tone. "Quinn, obviously you haven't thought through whatever this is about. And I'm not a psychic. I can't read your mind. Therefore, if you want me to place an ad for you—let me be clear—I need to know what it should say."

He glared at her, nodded and changed direction, heading back to his office. "I don't want to be disturbed." He shut the door quietly, but she suspected only pride had kept him from slamming it.

Not sixty seconds later Kimberly returned with a damp shirt and a wary look at Quinn's closed door. "What happened?"

"He's trying to find me." Maggie's voice sounded odd, even to her own ears.

"You mean the *you* of last night?"

"Yeah. I had to talk him out of buying a full-page ad in the newspaper. And billboards."

"Oh. My. God." Kimberly flopped into the chair opposite Maggie. "What are you going to do?"

Maggie giggled. She couldn't help it. "I'll do whatever he tells me to do. That's why I get paid the big bucks."

"Maggie!"

"What?"

"Come on. Don't you feel the least bit guilty? Even I could see he was...irritated."

"He'll get over it." Maggie shrugged, shoving away the twinge of nagging guilt. "I shouldn't feel guilty, should I? It's not like I forced him to do anything he didn't want to do."

"Right." Kimberly let that subject drop, but picked up another.

"And you don't want another night with him?"

"I didn't say that." Just the suggestion of experiencing more Quinn had her nerve endings jumping up and down and shouting *yes, yes, yes.* But Maggie knew all too well that risking more time with Quinn increased the danger of her getting caught. What she hadn't counted on was how very easily she could get caught up in the pleasure of a passionate venture.

"If screwing him out of your system in one night didn't work, you might want to go for another."

"Sheesh. I don't know how I feel yet." Except deliciously sated and ever so daring. She liked both feelings very much. And, for once, Maggie didn't want to think about the future. She just wanted to enjoy the parts of her plan that had worked. She still had her job. And she'd had her night of fun.

Kimberly swiped Maggie's coffee cup, sipped and frowned. "It's cold," she complained, then drained the rest in one long swallow. "So what are you going to do now?"

WHAT THE HELL WAS HE GOING to do? Thank God for Maggie's good sense or he'd be making a fool of himself with those billboards. He didn't know what he'd do without her, especially today when he was so distracted. He could count on Maggie to take care of the dog problem as well as a myriad of other details that he didn't have time for. She really had a brilliant future as a casting director and if he didn't rely on her so much in his office, he would have helped her on her way much sooner. Maggie was close to the perfect employee. She didn't ask him to find parts for her relatives in his movies, and while she nagged him about reading Kimberly's script, she did it because he ought to read his own production assistant's script. And Maggie had a way of reducing the chaos in his life and never asked for anything in return. She wouldn't even castigate him for ignoring the stack of messages on his desk while he paced his office, thinking.

He could hire a private investigator. Maybe a P.I. could lift the woman's prints off the hotel room balcony. After all, she'd gripped it tightly enough. But it was a hotel room and other tenants must have clutched that same balcony, although perhaps not quite for the same reason.

Damn her. Who did she think she was to pull a switch like that on him? He felt angry enough to charge into battle, but he hadn't a clue about his nemesis.

And he'd never been so intrigued by a woman in his life.

It would serve her right if he forgot she existed. Just chalk her up to one fantastic, mysterious experience. He should pretend to himself that he'd been drunk and had forgotten to ask her name. Pretend she hadn't struck some chord that made him yearn to beat her at her own game. But to do that, he had to learn her identity—preferably without making a fool of himself in front of Maggie and the entire population of Hollywood.

Although his loyal secretary hadn't a clue what had happened, he could just imagine her smirk of amusement if she knew that a woman had placed her boss in such an untenable predicament—no way would he reveal a smidgeon of the intimate, embarrassing details. Not only had the mystery woman not asked him for anything, but she'd given him the best sex he'd ever had and walked away without telling him her name. As if what they'd shared wasn't worth a repeat performance.

Damn. Damn. Damn.

Quinn dropped into his chair and swiveled to face the window and stare out into the city. Hundreds of people on the streets of L.A. were going about their everyday business. He should be taking care of his.

Instead he was obsessed with that woman.

He kept going over the facts that might clue him in to her identity.

She'd arrived in the company limo and stayed in the room paid for by the studio. He picked up the phone and dialed the company driver himself. "Charles, was there anything unusual about your pickup of Laine Lamonde?"

"No, sir. Unless..."

"Unless what?"

"I thought it a bit odd that she wore her mask the entire time, sir."

"Thank you, Charles."

Another dead end.

There were no credit card bills to trace. No phone calls. Not even a note. Studying the paparazzi photographs of the masked woman didn't give him any clues, either.

No one had seen her face. Not the limo driver, the magazine photographers, the other party guests. Not even him.

He could run into her at lunch, or out jogging, or in the elevator and he'd never recognize her. She'd given him so little to go on. They hadn't even discussed anything as personal as her favorite drink.

His intercom buzzed. "What?"

Maggie still sounded as if she were chuckling. "Poopsy just ate the director's wig."

"And?" He didn't need interruptions right now. Hadn't he told her that he didn't want to be disturbed?

"Poopsy's tummy is upset. Rege wants to take her to the vet, which will stop production for the day, since they need new dialogue written."

Stopping would mean hundreds of thousands of dollars in cost overruns. Filming a movie took dozens of people, actors and actresses, stunt people, cameramen, grips, cosmeticians, wardrobe and sound people. They couldn't shut down because one mutt had an upset tummy.

"Can't they phone the vet?"

"Apparently he won't diagnose over the phone."

"Maggie, what's that liquid substance that makes little kids vomit?"

"Ipecac syrup?"

"Yeah. Tell them to give some to the dog."

"Suppose it kills him?"

"Check with the vet. Pay him his walk-in fee. But don't let them shut down."

"Okay. Oh, if you want a full-page ad in tomorrow's paper, I need the copy within the next hour."

He released the intercom button. There had to be a way to word the ad other than "Producer seeks mystery woman wearing mask for another night of hot sex." He groaned in frustration that his thought processes couldn't seem to deal with this problem in a logical manner. He'd started his career by writing screenplays, surely he could come up with something subtly worded. But then, if he made the wording too vague, his mystery woman might not get it. And if he was specific—too many people would realize what had happened to him. Normally when he had a writing problem he had an entire studio full of high-paid writers whom he could put to work on a solution. But using them would mean explaining his awkward predicament, and then he'd likely be reading about his love life in tomorrow's gossip column.

Right now only the mystery woman knew what had happened, and Quinn wanted to keep it that way. But he considered confiding in Maggie. While Maggie might chuckle at him, his secretary knew her job depended on keeping her mouth shut.

Maggie wouldn't gossip, except maybe to Kimberly. And Kimberly wouldn't dare repeat his problems if she ever wanted to work in this town again.

Quinn strummed his fingers on his desk. Talking to Maggie might be his best bet. She was a woman. She knew how they thought.

And he had an idea. Quinn shot out of his chair and his office, back toward Maggie's desk. He waited impatiently for her to finish what sounded like a conference call with the vet and the writer.

She spoke calmly into the phone as if she dealt with animal emergencies and temperamental writers every day. "You got that, Rege? Feed the dog regular food and bread. Anything the animal swallowed should pass right through."

The moment Maggie hung up the phone, Quinn had to refrain from pouncing. "Who signed the receipt for the jewels Laine was supposed to wear?"

"The hotel concierge."

"And where are the jewels now?"

MAGGIE OPENED A DRAWER and handed him a faxed receipt from the jewelry store that had loaned the necklace and earrings. "The jewelry was returned by courier. Why?"

"Because the woman who impersonated Laine wore these jewels last night."

"Someone impersonated Laine?" Maggie widened her eyes in surprise, thinking if she could pull this off then she deserved an Academy Award.

"And she wore the necklace and earrings delivered to Laine at the hotel."

Maggie frowned at Quinn. "Are you sure?"

He glared at her. "She was with me for hours and wore nothing but the jewelry. I'm sure."

Under his fierce scowl, Maggie swallowed hard. "You're saying that someone sneaked into Laine's hotel room, borrowed these jewels, wore them while she was with you and then returned them to the jewelry store? Really Quinn. I'm not sure if you're saying someone pulled one over on you, but if she did, would she have returned millions of dollars in jewels?"

"Maybe I should have hotel security check their video cams."

Quinn no longer sounded so sure. Obviously he didn't want to create a fuss and reveal that he'd been duped. Maggie didn't blame him. Luckily all the hotel security cams would reveal was Kimberly in Laine's room, but Kimberly had been sent there by Quinn to deliver the dress, and when she'd left, she'd hidden the dress in a shopping bag. Time to give him a graceful way out.

"You know almost every jewelry store has to deal with knockoffs. I'll bet the woman who deceived you bought black-market fakes at the corner kiosk."

Quinn eyed her oddly. "But how would this woman have known what Laine would wear?"

Maggie had never expected Quinn to react to last night in any way but casual. Now he was questioning her as if he suspected someone in the office might have been his mystery woman. But they both knew that too many people worked in Simitar Studios for him to begin narrowing down the possibilities. Costuming alone employed several hundred people. And his office personnel included another few hundred if he included secretaries, clerks, assistants, messengers and cleaning people. Most likely he'd figure that the woman he'd been with was an aspiring actress and that could mean any one of thousands of women who came into contact through the studio's network of casting agents. If he included people at the jewelry store and the press, he couldn't even begin a rational search.

Still, her stomach churned. What was she going to do? She had to think fast to lead him in a different direction.

Maggie shrugged to hide her breathless surprise. "Maybe someone in wardrobe mentioned the jewelry to her hairdresser who mentioned it to her mother who told the neighbor—you know how it is. Or maybe the jewelry store sent the items out ahead of time to be photographed for a fashion shoot, hoping to capitalize on extra publicity with Laine wearing them. You want me to ask around?"

"No."

"This other woman really made you think you were with Laine?" Maggie probed.

Quinn didn't answer her question. Instead he tossed the faxed receipt back to Maggie. "I need to find her."

"Why?" she asked, playing all innocentlike, but very, very curious. Carefully she placed the receipt back into her drawer. "Do you want to sign her for your next movie?"

Quinn's eyes burned a hot green flame. "This is personal."

"Oh." As his secretary, she had to back off. But

she hoped he'd continue. She especially wanted to learn how he felt about *her*.

Quinn spoke in a burst of speed. "If you must know, she was a great lover."

"Really?" Maggie didn't have to feign fascination this time. "What did she do?"

Quinn threaded his hand through his hair, looking sexy in his distress. But then all the man had to do to look sexy was breathe. "That's the hell of it. I don't know exactly why I can't get her out of my mind."

"Next you'll be telling me you're in love," she teased, trying to lighten the moment.

"I don't believe in love," Quinn snapped.

Maggie let out a long, low sigh and shook her head. "You've never loved anyone? What about your parents?"

"That's different. Sex isn't involved."

"So if you have sex with someone, you can't love them. That's a theory I've never heard before. Did you learn that on Jerry Springer or just make it up?"

Quinn frowned at her. "Why are we having this discussion?"

"Because you're confused." Maggie teased him again, sensing that if she gave him one ounce of pity, he'd retreat into anger. "Because you need my good sense to set you straight?" She held her breath, wondering if he'd retreat to his office again.

Instead he flopped in the chair opposite her desk. "I suppose you believe in love at first sight?"

"Why not? My father claims he fell in love with

my mother in the fifth grade. Three kids, five grand-kids and forty years later, they're still in love.''

''That's bizarre.'' Quinn spoke matter-of-factly, his expression as doubtful as if she'd told him to believe in a fairy tale.

She supposed her parents' long-term relationship sounded odd from his Hollywood perspective. Many celebrities replaced marriage partners more often than they did their cars. Yet, however much fun he made of her middle-class Michigan upbringing, she had her own values and her own sense of self-worth.

''Sleeping with a woman whose name you don't know is bizarre,'' she countered, and watched him flush.

''I thought she was Laine Lamonde.''

''But even while you still believed she was Laine, you never thought you loved her, right?''

''Of course not.''

''So why can't you just chalk up the night to a great experience and let it go? The lady obviously doesn't want to be found.''

''What about what *I* want?'' Quinn countered. ''I mean, she just dropped into my life, then disappeared. What kind of woman would do that?''

''Oh, come on, Quinn. How many times have you gone out with a woman and then never seen her again?''

''That's different.''

''Why?''

''Because usually when that happens, it's a busi-ness date. You know that. The woman knows that. The women don't expect anything except a little publicity and maybe a part in my next film. Most of the time, we don't even kiss good-night.''

Maggie hadn't known anything of the sort. All those times she'd arranged for his car, his dinner reservation, she'd longingly wanted to take the place of his date.

She'd always figured Quinn got the girl in bed. ''What about all those hotel reservations that you had me make?''

''For publicity. Nothing more.''

Quinn took most of those women out for appearance's sake? Apparently he wasn't the playboy he seemed. And his revelation floored her.

Quinn wasn't a playboy.

She tried the thought on for size and oddly found that it fit. Quinn's business relationships lasted for years. He'd used the same accountant and lawyers for the past decade. He had certain directors that usually became his friends—long-term friends. And despite his unstable childhood, he remained in contact with both of his parents.

When he'd taken out one woman after another, she'd just assumed he was a playboy—instead, he hadn't been interested enough to ask the women out again. Yet, Quinn wasn't a monk, either. He'd engaged in two longer relationships since she'd worked for him. And he certainly knew his way around a bedroom—he'd more than proven that to her.

She spoke more sympathetically. ''You still haven't told me why last night was so special.''

''I don't know.''

''I think you do.''

"I said that I don't know."

"I know what you said."

A silence between them grew while he appeared to be thinking hard, probably back over their evening. And she couldn't help wondering if he remembered their time together so very much differently than she did. The air between them had seemed electrified. Rarified.

And she waited for Quinn to figure it out, wondering if he saw himself clearly enough to be able to do so.

"She didn't want anything from me. She even returned the jewels."

He hadn't given her the answer she'd expected. She'd thought if he spoke at all, he'd mention the act of making love, not the reason behind the act.

"Excuse me? This woman wanted sex from you, right?"

"She didn't ask for a part in my movies. She didn't ask me to read a script she'd written. She didn't ask for gossip to print in tomorrow's paper or an introduction or—"

"She wanted you." Maggie finally got it. "And only you."

"It was incredibly…flattering."

"And that's why losing her is so hard," Maggie realized, sympathy entering her tone, reflecting her feelings.

Quinn's voice grew tight with determination. "I'll find her."

At the fierceness of his tone, a tiny shock of apprehension shivered down Maggie's spine. She'd never expected Quinn to be so affected by last night's fling. In actuality, she hadn't thought about his feelings at all. One of the reasons Quinn was so wrong for Maggie was that she wanted a man who came from a stable background. And she'd never pegged a man who had starlets at his beck and call as anyone who would think of their time together as anything but an erotic interlude.

She figured that for him the night would not be so different from any other night. That she wouldn't be so different from any of the other women he went out with. For him, the night should have been a lark, a good time, a fond but fleeting memory.

Before she'd impersonated Laine, she'd wondered whether she was fooling herself. If making love with him one time would be enough to set her craving for him aside. She still didn't know. Her feelings were jumbled inside her. She needed time to sort out what to do, where to go from here.

So this entire conversation with Quinn seemed unreal. She didn't know how she felt, and it was ironic that he'd come to her for advice and to vent.

For the first time, Maggie wondered if she'd made a mess of things. She looked up into the harsh determination in Quinn's eyes and forced herself to speak. "If you found her, if she was here in the room with you right now instead of me, what would you say to her?"

"It doesn't matter."

"Of course it matters."

"Not until I find her."

"And how are you going to do that?"

"I don't know, but she must work in the industry. She knew Laine was coming and that she canceled her plans to be with me. She knew what dress Laine would be wearing. She even wore the right jewelry. All that information had to come from an inside source. She obviously went to a lot of trouble. But why?"

"Perhaps, you'll find her and ask her," Maggie offered, for lack of anything useful to say. She couldn't give him her reasons without giving herself away, not when she had so much else to think about.

The telephone rang, interrupting their conversation. It was Mia, an actress and former friend of Quinn's who'd married and moved to Vancouver. She placed the woman on hold, curious to see what Quinn would do. "It's Mia."

He sighed. "Tell her I'll call her back."

Maggie did as he asked, wondering if he wanted to avoid talking to the woman, or if he preferred a more private time to talk with her. She couldn't read Quinn—his expressionless features told her nothing. She didn't like that he could so easily close off his thoughts to her—especially after what they'd shared.

She'd set up their night together as a one-time event, but that was before she'd known Quinn could be so affected by her. Before she'd known that Quinn was not the playboy she'd assumed him to be. And while her plan had worked out even better than she'd anticipated, the repercussions boggled her mind.

What was she going to do?

What did she want to do? Have another go-round with Quinn without revealing her identity?

Oh, yeah.

But was that even possible? She didn't know yet. Right now she could only be sure that their time together had been spectacular. And way too short. Was she becoming addicted to the danger, to the risk or to him? While long-term was out of the question, since he wasn't the kind of man who'd ever settle down— judging from his parents' histories and his own lack of commitment to any woman—she certainly wouldn't mind an encore, and from the looks and sound of him, he wouldn't, either. In fact, he seemed even more impatient and eager than she could have ever hoped.

Quinn scowled in obvious frustration. After all he'd thrown at her, Maggie needed to be alone to think and digest. Yet, it was her nature to try to make things better, and she couldn't stop herself from offering Quinn hope.

"Quinn, maybe she had such a good time that she'll find you."

6

QUINN REMAINED IN MAGGIE'S office as the phone rang again. He should return to work, but he was reluctant to leave this conversation without some answers. Maggie hadn't been as helpful as he'd hoped.

Maggie picked up the phone. "Simitar Studios. Quinn Scott's office."

She listened intently, then hung up the phone. "We have a problem."

"What?"

"Laine Lamonde flew her Boston terrier, Molly, over here two months ago. The dog should have been released from quarantine today. It wasn't."

"And this is my problem because?"

"Laine's agent says she would so appreciate it if you could rescue her dog—"

"Send Kimberly."

"Can't." Maggie grinned at him. "I'm afraid this may take your silver-smooth tongue."

"Why can't Kimberly—"

"Because only the owner or the owner's representative can pick up the dog." The fax machine beeped. "The power of attorney is coming through right now. It's in your name."

Quinn swallowed a string of curses. What was it

with him and dog problems? He didn't even own a pet. He figured it wasn't fair to keep an animal and then not be there for it—it was the same philosophy that kept him from considering ever having a wife.

"How long has the dog been in quarantine?"

"Two months. Why?"

"Would it be cruel to make her wait another day?"

"I suspect Molly would be fine but do you want to disappoint Laine?"

He sighed. "You've got a point. I'll need you to come with me."

"Me?"

"You don't expect me to steer the car *and* hold the mutt do you?"

"I could order a limo for you."

"I don't think so. I need to drive—I think best behind the wheel."

Quinn waited for Maggie to cancel his appointments and to arrange to have his calls answered by the service. That done, he escorted her out of the building into the humid sunshine. He actually enjoyed the ride through the city. In the middle of the day, traffic was light and he found driving on L.A.'s freeways pleasant—not a common sentiment.

Maggie didn't chatter. He liked that about her. She respected that he had things on his mind and didn't pry. Yet, if he'd wanted to talk, she would have accommodated his wishes. He'd been lucky to inherit the perfect secretary and reminded himself that he really should get the studio to give her a raise.

They arrived at the quarantine section and showed his identification to the woman in charge. Tall, black, overweight and world-weary, she fingered the power-of-attorney paperwork. "Is this a fax?"

"Yes, ma'am." Quinn smiled at her but his charm didn't make a dent in the woman's frown.

"Faxes aren't legally binding."

"Says who?"

"My boss. If you want to yell at him, he's two doors down that corridor, then take your first left and it's the second door on the right."

Her boss, skinny, short and bald with thick eyeglasses took one look at the fax and shook his head. "No can do. You're wasting my time and yours."

Quinn was about to step forward and pummel the desk in frustration, when Maggie shook her head slightly and sent him a let-me-handle-this look. "Excuse me, sir. Do you know that this Boston terrier belongs to Laine Lamonde?"

"Never heard of her."

"This man is director Quinn Scott—"

"Never heard of him, either."

"But you've heard of Jason Scott, haven't you?" Maggie tried again, her tone a model of patience.

Quinn shifted from foot to foot. If the man hadn't heard of Jason Scott, they should quit while they were behind.

"Sure I heard of him. Jason Scott's a film legend."

"Well, this man is his son and the woman whose dog he's trying to pick up is starring in his next film. We might be able to arrange for you and your wife to attend the premier if you could help us."

The man peered at Quinn. "I do see a family resemblance."

Quinn bit back another comment. He really didn't want to spoil Maggie's efforts on his behalf.

"And this lady that he's trying to help out is still in France. Plane trouble. She's really worried about her dog."

Was Maggie laying it on too thick? No. She had the petty bureaucrat practically eating out of her hand.

He actually winked at Maggie. "Well, you know what they say?"

"What?"

"Rules is made to be broken."

Quinn refrained from wincing. He didn't consider himself a snob, but as a writer he hated to hear the English language mangled so badly.

He pulled out a form, filled in the dog's name, Laine's name and copied Quinn's driver's license number onto it, then stamped it. "Here take this back to Mandy. You're all set."

"Thank you for the help." Maggie picked up one of the man's business cards. "We won't forget."

Except they weren't all set quite yet. Mandy took the form and gave it to a Hispanic girl with large brown eyes and a wistful smile. She promised to bring the dog to them in a jiffy.

Thirty minutes later they were still waiting. Quinn hated dealing with bureaucracy. That's what assistants were for. Between his aggravation over Laine's impersonator and dealing with dog problems, his patience was wearing thin. Other people had come and gone with their pets, but there was no sign of a Boston terrier named Molly.

Maggie approached Mandy again. "Ma'am. I was wondering if you could check—"

"You people are still here?"

Quinn barely bit back a sigh. If the woman had once looked away from her computer screen over the counter, they would have been in plain sight.

Maggie upped the volume of her voice. "I'm so worried about this dog. You haven't lost her, have you?"

Behind them, other people who waited to claim their animals heard her and frowned. Behind the counter, dogs in cages barked and birds cooed. The odors didn't help Quinn's bad mood.

"Perhaps, we should go see your boss again?" Maggie suggested just a little too sweetly. Watching her play onto the other woman's fears was just a little too satisfying. He'd always known Maggie was good at manipulating people, that trait made her a good secretary. For a moment Quinn even wondered how often she manipulated him.

But then the Hispanic girl slid around the corner and hurried over. She whispered in Mandy's ear. "We can't find the dog."

"What do you mean?" Maggie didn't even try to pretend that she hadn't been eavesdropping.

"We can't locate the animal."

Maggie raised her voice just a bit louder. "Does that mean the animal never arrived in this building? That she's lost here? Or that you gave the dog to someone else by accident?"

"We don't make those kinds of mistakes," Mandy

spoke primly, but Quinn caught a glimpse of fear in her eyes.

"Good. Then produce the animal and we shall be on our way."

An hour later, the best explanation they could come up with was the dog might have accidentally been included in a lot that went to a dog breeder in Ojai, a small tourist town about an hour north of Los Angeles.

With his day already shot, Quinn decided to drive out there. They now had a picture of the animal. She was so ugly she was cute. Her big brown eyes, pug nose and black and white markings should make it possible to distinguish her from other Boston terriers, but Quinn was secretly hoping that the breeder would help them out here.

However, once they arrived at the one-acre lot, he found the breeder apologetic. "It's hard to tell them apart—unless it's your own dog."

Great.

Maggie stroked a puppy, allowing it to lick under her chin. "Did you receive the correct number of dogs in your last shipment?"

"Yes. I'm sorry. I've already sold them but I can give you names and addresses."

"You wouldn't happen to have pictures?" Maggie asked.

"I'm afraid not."

Once they were back in the car, Quinn turned off the radio. "You don't suppose we could phone each of those people, have them e-mail us a picture of their dog—"

"—and ask Laine if one of them happens to be hers?'' Maggie let out a long sigh. "I don't think that's a good idea. Besides most people don't have digital cameras and scanners and—"

"Okay. Okay. Now what?"

"Could we stop and eat something? I'm starved.''

"Sorry. You should have said something earlier.'' Quinn could really be insensitive sometimes. Especially when he got wrapped up in his work. Or wrapped up in solving a mystery. He didn't want to be chasing all over California for clues about Laine's dog. He wanted to be looking for the person who had made love to him. But he had fewer clues about her than he did about Molly. At least the dog had a name. His mystery woman didn't.

QUINN WASN'T SULKING, he was brooding. He'd wasted the day looking for Laine's missing dog and canceled his date for the movie premiere he was supposed to attend that evening. Instead he took another long drive to clear his head. Could Laine Lamonde have set him up? He couldn't discount any possibilities no matter how improbable, but what would have been the star's motive?

That was the burning question. Why would any woman have acted like his mystery woman? Quinn even considered whether a friend or a rival could have sent a prostitute. But why? Although Quinn had never paid for sex, he believed that the woman he'd been with at Hotel Vendaz had been way too creative, too personal and into lovemaking to be a pro. He hadn't imagined that electric tension between them. Besides,

Quinn had a reputation as a ladies' man and none of his friends were into practical jokes. And surely if it was a prank, the jokester would have come clean by now.

Nothing made sense.

When his cell phone rang, he checked the caller ID to see the caller's identity. Maggie. "What's up?"

"I found Molly."

"Where?"

"Those idiots sent her to Laine's address—at the studio. She's been with the animals on that Halloween movie we're filming."

"Good work."

"Thanks. Laine's agent wants me to send her to—"

"Just do it. And thanks, Maggie."

The moment he hung up, his cell phone rang again. This time the caller identification had been blocked. He answered out of habit more than a desire to speak to anyone. "Quinn here."

"Bonjour."

It was her! The woman whose name he still didn't know. Elation seared through his excitement, and Quinn pulled onto the shoulder of the road.

A million questions zipped through his mind, like asking her name, or how she'd gotten his private number, or if she really had a French accent or needed to conceal her real identity—especially since that would mean he knew this woman. But he didn't want to frighten her away with the third degree. He kept his tone casual. "I'm glad you called."

"Really?"

He sensed her hesitation, as if she might hang up if he said one wrong thing. He needed to keep her talking. He just hoped his expert negotiation and people skills didn't let him down. "I enjoyed being with you."

"We were good together, yes?"

"Yes." *Were?* He didn't like her speaking in the past tense. As if they had no future. No possibility of another date. He clutched the phone, determined to change her mind. Determined not to lose the best thing that had happened to him in such a long time. Right now he felt so alive, every sense so alert, that the air he breathed seemed fresher, as if filled with crazed ions like the crisp air before a storm.

He sensed that she might hang up at any moment, that this connection was fragile. He held his breath, waiting for her to make the next move. She didn't. Why had she called? He knew better than to ask so direct a question or he might frighten her away. An indirect method might be best. Was she wondering if it was safe to meet him in person? Would she consider allowing him to take her to dinner?

He didn't think so. Last night she'd come to him wearing a mask. Now he couldn't see her at all and she'd blocked her phone number so he couldn't return her call. Clearly she still wanted to keep her identity secret.

"What are you wearing?" he asked.

She hesitated. Had his somewhat off-the-wall question and change in conversation taken her completely by surprise? Was she dressed for dinner? Ready for dancing? Or a night on the town?

"I'm wearing bubbles."

"Bubbles?"

"I'm taking a bath. And the slick bubbles on my bare skin made me think of you."

No doubt, just as she intended, his mouth went dry at the thought of her naked flesh covered with frothy bubbles. "You called the right man."

"I did?"

Quinn was now in his element. He loved to make deals, but first he had to set the bait. "You remember how I played with your breasts with my palms last night?"

"Yes."

"I want you to play with yourself just like that."

This time, she didn't hesitate. "Hold on. Let me put you on speakerphone so both of my hands are free."

Water splashed and he imagined the ripples of water parting the bubbles, her pink nipples peeking through white foam. And he immediately grew rockhard, his slacks tightening uncomfortably. Still, he had to wonder at how easily she'd accepted his suggestion. She'd called him. Was she setting him up to make a fool of him?

"Can you hear me?" she asked.

"Just fine." He considered his next words carefully, and concluded that he could live with the consequences if his statement somehow became public. "Are your hands on your breasts?"

"Hmm. My hands are softer than yours."

"Pinch your nipples," he ordered.

"Mmm."

"Keep your hands on your breasts." He had no trouble issuing orders. Although he'd never done anything like this in his life, he knew exactly what he wanted her to do next. Now that he had her thinking about sex, he switched the subject. "Are you taping this conversation?"

She chuckled. "*Non.* I assure you that if our conversation became public, I would have much more to lose than you would."

"And why is that?"

"Because you are a powerful man." Water swished in the background but he heard no other clues to her location. No traffic. Or airplanes. Not even a dog barking. "And a Hollywood scandal would only enhance your reputation. But I could lose my job."

He had to use every ounce of control to refrain from asking her where she worked. Probably for him, he guessed, since she knew his schedule and phone number.

"Where are your hands?" he asked her.

"On my breasts, exactly where you suggested."

He almost groaned aloud at the image. But he kept to his agenda. "I'd like us to make a bargain."

She didn't reply to his suggestion. Like an expert negotiator, she distracted him. "My nipples are quite tight and hard. And I'm tingly all over. Perhaps, I should hang up."

Why is it that God gave man a brain and a penis and not enough blood to service both at the same time? Since all the blood in his body seemed to have gone south, he was having more difficulty than usual keeping the conversation on track.

On the upside, he hadn't scared her off. So he pressed a little more. "I'm going to give you a very pleasant hour over the phone and you'll give me something in return."

"I will?"

"Tomorrow, visit me in my office," he suggested, praying she wouldn't hang up.

A long silence hung in the phone connection between them.

Finally she spoke. "Tell me why you want us to meet again."

His heart rate accelerated. The writer in him knew what he said next might be the last thing he ever said to her. He mentally rejected one line after another. And finally settled on the truth. "The sex was wonderful, but I want more from you."

"More?"

"You've caught my attention," he admitted. "I can't stop thinking about you." Had he gone too far? Or not far enough?

"I like you thinking about me. So I agree to your terms." He pumped his fist in success.

"But I have one condition of my own."

"Which is?"

She chuckled, a rich, deep sound that shot straight to his core. "Such impatience. Tomorrow, I'll send you a gift. And it will be up to you whether or not to accept that gift in the manner I've asked."

So vague. So mysterious. What was she up to? He knew better than to ask. Dared not push her any harder. So he took what she'd offered.

The air eased out of his lungs with a breath of elation. She would meet him tomorrow. ''Then we have a deal.''

MAGGIE HAD NEVER HAD PHONE SEX before. She'd certainly never watched in a mirror as she brought herself to climax, either. But just hearing Quinn's sexy voice in her ear had done strange things to her psyche. Suddenly her secretary persona had been left behind and she'd blossomed into this boldly sexual woman who knew what she wanted and knew how to get it.

Maggie had hung up the phone, liking this emerging bombshell part of herself. First, it was fun. Second, she had been having the best sex of her life. And third, she found that her knack for planning was allowing her the opportunity for additional trysts.

She fully intended to keep her word and visit him tomorrow in his office. It wouldn't matter if he arranged to have his office watched. She wouldn't even have to evade the security cameras to enact the plan that had popped into her head fully blown as she'd agreed to Quinn's bargain. As long as she kept her identity secret, as long as nothing went wrong with her outrageous scheme, she wouldn't lose her job. And now that Quinn had admitted that he was thinking about her quite a bit, she felt even more secure about her role in this game she was playing with Quinn.

However, her nerves were frazzled at her audacity. But the excitement and the risk of discovery kept egging her on. She was so keyed up, so jazzed by the risks, that she wondered if living on the edge could become addictive.

That she'd stirred Quinn's interest excited her enough to risk another encounter. The sex had been wonderful, but when Quinn had told her that he wanted more, her heart had clenched, quivered and filled with hope that maybe her one-night stand could turn into a full-fledged fling.

So what if women threw themselves at him on a daily basis? So what if he came from a background that made it impossible for him to believe in love? She wasn't even considering anything permanent—in fact, that kind of thinking was fatal when it came to Quinn. Quinn was heat and pleasure and oh-so temporary—which simply added to the exhilaration.

After taking her shower, she planned to go straight to bed. She hadn't slept at all last night and snuggling into her covers after being so physically sated was irresistible. But the moment she belted her bathrobe, Maggie heard knocking at her front door.

Her pulse skyrocketed. Quinn couldn't have found her, she told herself. She'd blocked the call before dialing his number. And she'd continued to use the phony accent to disguise her voice, hadn't she?

Yet, her friends didn't come by without calling. Her family lived fifteen hundred miles away in Michigan and never paid her unexpected visits. Her best friend Leslie was out of town researching water skiing on Lake Powell for a trendy travel magazine and… *Just answer the door, Maggie.*

She checked the peephole first.

Kimberly? What was she doing here on a Tuesday

night? Tuesday night! Yikes. They were supposed to have met downstairs about ten minutes ago to attend a play given by the UCLA drama department. Maggie liked to watch the up-and-coming actors and actresses for talent and had especially wanted to see Serena Kendall again, a grad student who oozed sex appeal and talent in her second leading role. Kimberly enjoyed viewing creative efforts of college writers who only had shoestring budgets to work with.

Maggie opened her door. "I'm so sorry. I totally forgot."

Kimberly checked her watch. "If you hurry and dress we can still make it."

Maggie didn't want to cancel on her friend. She didn't like women who abandoned their girlfriends every time there was a new man in their life. At the same time, she didn't have the energy to dress, let alone stay up another four hours.

Maggie shook her head. "Would you mind if I don't go? I'm so tired I can barely keep my eyes open."

Kimberly peered at her. "You don't have some man stashed in the bedroom, do you?"

"I wish. But no, why?"

"Because your skin is positively glowing with that I'm-so-sated look."

"Does phone sex count?"

Kimberly walked straight into Maggie's kitchen, opened the fridge and helped herself to a beer. She twisted off the top, took a deep swig, then settled into a kitchen chair. "Your life sounds much more interesting than the play. Tell me you called Quinn."

"I called Quinn."

"And?"

If Maggie hadn't been so confused, she would never have admitted what she'd done. But now that she had, she didn't mind. She needed someone to talk to. Kimberly would understand, and she might need her help again tomorrow.

"Quinn knows I'm not Laine, but he doesn't know that I'm Maggie."

Kimberly grinned. "You know, it worries me that I actually understood that convoluted sentence."

"You want to talk about my grammar or my sex life?" Maggie filled up a glass with ice water and sat at the table across from Kimberly.

"Look, I was all for a glorious one-nighter. But aren't you pushing your luck?"

"I agreed to meet with him tomorrow. In person."

"You may have an invisible *S* on your chest, but you aren't stupid."

"I have a plan."

Kimberly shook her head and sipped her beer. "You're playing with fire and you're going to get burned."

"Hey, you were the one who encouraged me in the first place," Maggie reminded her. "I was hoping you could help me out tomorrow by answering Quinn's phone. I'll call in sick."

Kimberly shook her head. "I don't know which calls to put through to Quinn and who to stall."

"I'll make you a list."

"Am I putting my career on the line here?"

"Of course not."

"If Quinn finds out who you are and that I'm helping you…" Kimberly shuddered. "He'll fire us both."

"Me, maybe, but not you. I'll tell him that you had no idea what was going on." What Maggie didn't mention to her friend was that she wasn't just doing this for herself. She was offering Quinn something he'd never had before—a woman who wanted him for himself and not for what he could give her. And even if she was taking an incredible risk, she couldn't resist giving his ego a boost. "Quinn might get angry, but he's fair. You'll be okay."

"I don't know."

"If you want Quinn to produce your movie, you need to make contacts, and there's no better way to make those contacts than to answer Quinn's phones."

"Quinn scares me. He's so intense. He makes me nervous. I always spill coffee or trip or do dumb things around him. It's bad enough that he thinks I'm a klutz but—"

"Stop making excuses. You encouraged me and now you can't back out. Besides, I promised to show up and I can't pull this off without you to cover the phones and the door."

"And why won't he recognize you this time?"

"Quinn will be screening his new movie in his office tomorrow."

"So?"

"He'll be alone."

"So?"

"It'll be dark."

"So?"

Maggie had no intention of telling her friend her entire plan. Some things were private. Kimberly didn't need to know the intimate details. "If the lights are all out, he won't be able to see my face."

Kimberly slugged back her beer, set down the empty bottle and spun it between her fingers. "You're going to seduce him in his office?"

"That's why I need you. No phone calls. No interruptions."

"And then what?"

Maggie frowned. "What do you mean, 'and then what?' Then I leave and—"

"What will you do the next time?" Kimberly asked.

"I'll think of something."

Kimberly sighed. "The more seductions that you set up, the greater the chance that you're going to get caught."

"I'll be careful."

"Stop thinking with your hormones and use your head. Suppose he checks with security?"

"He'll only learn that his mystery woman works in the building or had a guest pass. Of course, I'll be there after I call in sick, but he still won't know that it's me."

Kimberly sipped her beer. "Suppose he turns on the lights?"

"He doesn't really want to know who I am."

Kimberly rolled her eyes. "And how do you know?"

"Because he likes the game. He told me he was glad I called him. And he doesn't want our encounters to—pardon the pun—come to an end any more than I do or he wouldn't have suggested that we meet tomorrow.''

Maggie pulled out all the stops. She opened a kitchen cabinet, removed a box of Godiva's chocolate-dipped apricots and pushed them across the table. ''So, will you do it?''

7

QUINN ENTERED SIMITAR STUDIO the next morning
completely out of sorts. After the stimulating phone
conversation with his mystery woman, he couldn't
sleep. Restless, on edge, he'd spent most of the night
tossing and turning. He'd never been this turned on
by any woman. Never been this distracted from his
work. Never been so worked up over a woman that
he had trouble falling asleep. Finally, early in the
morning, he'd slid into a deep slumber only to have
his mother phone from Africa to ask if he had work
for her on a new film when she returned.

Already late, Quinn had showered in haste, wondering if his mystery lady would fulfill her promise
to him today. Usually he could count on the studio's
security to keep out intruders, but he suspected that
she worked at Simitar Studios. Unfortunately
thousands of people worked in the building and he
didn't know them all.

Quinn wondered if the woman was playing him.
Could she be wrapping him in a web of sexual intrigue only to ask him for something later? As much
as the thought bothered him, he'd been around long
enough to know that whatever demand she eventually

might put to him that he could always say no. And in the meantime, he intended to enjoy himself.

Despite his lack of sleep, Quinn was eager to face the day, eager to meet any surprises his secretive lover threw his way. So he wasn't as perturbed as he normally would have been to find Maggie nowhere in sight, and Kimberly sitting behind his secretary's desk.

"Good morning, Mr. Scott," Kimberly spoke to him, one hand covering the phone's mouthpiece.

"Where's Maggie?" Quinn asked, after nodding a greeting.

"Sick. I'm filling in."

Not good. Quinn sipped a triple espresso, suspecting he'd need the extra caffeine kick without Maggie in the office to run interference. Of all the days she had to be out, why did it have to be today? If his lover showed, Quinn would have preferred competent Maggie sitting behind the desk to cover for him.

Maggie always had the extraordinary ability to keep him organized, not easy when he couldn't predict what he'd be doing from one minute to the next. "Any messages?"

Kimberly reached for the stack, knocked them over and paper fluttered like fall leaves in a winter wind. "Oops. Sorry." She scrambled on hands and knees to pick up the messages.

"I'll be at my desk." Quinn carried his coffee into his office before she spilled it—and before he opened his mouth and said something about her clumsiness. Normally Quinn might have been amused that every time he met with his very capable production assistant she turned into an accident waiting to happen. But today, he'd have preferred for his office phones to be answered smoothly and efficiently.

He had work to do. Instead of asking Kimberly to patch him through to John Davis, he dialed himself.

The talented director picked up on the first ring. "Hey, Quinn. Can I call you back? I'm two weeks behind schedule and five million over budget."

"So why do you sound so happy?"

John cooed. "I am *soooo* in *loooove.*"

"Gracie—" Quinn knew the actress and John's leading lady well "—is looking hot?"

"She and Bontiki create a chemistry together that's igniting the screen."

Since John's current film was another of Quinn's projects, he couldn't have been more pleased. The budget overrun had been foreseen, as had the extra days of shooting. "What do you think of Laine Lamonde?"

"Don't know her. Heard she's a prima donna with a capital *P.* Hey, dust her, don't bury her." Quinn realized that John was talking to someone on the set, not him, before the director said, "Sorry, Quinn. Fairy dust doesn't agree with our poor Gracie who wears contact lenses."

"We need to talk about your next project."

"Have you signed Laine?"

"Her plane had mechanical trouble. She should be here soon."

"Shit. Gracie looks like a freaking ghost. She's a fairy, damn it." J.D. switched back to Quinn. "And the male lead?"

"That's why we need to talk."

"Okay. We wrap around nine. Meet me for drinks at ten? You're buying."

"Ten, it is." Quinn typed the appointment into his PDA and told it to flash reminders at him on the hour, every hour, starting at seven.

The moment he hung up, Kimberly buzzed him. "Mr. Scott?"

"Yes?"

"You want me to bring in your messages now?"

"Sure." Unless she expected them to fly in here by themselves.

Kimberly opened his door, scooted inside without tripping over her own feet, walked across the desk and placed the messages on his desk.

"Thank—"

A loud clatter sounded as the reels of film that she'd been carrying under her arm dropped and rolled onto his desk. And knocked over his coffee, spilling over his messages.

"Sorry. So sorry."

Quinn jerked back before the coffee slopped on his suit, then tossed a few napkins onto the spill. "Would you relax?"

"How can I relax when you are the most important person in my life?"

"Excuse me?" His head jerked up and his eyes narrowed. Kimberly had him going for a minute there, but no way could she be his mystery woman. Her hair was dark and long enough to hit her waist. She was slender and feminine, tidy. His mystery woman was curvier, taller and, most of all, she had a boldness about her that Kimberly could never carry off, at least not without a few more years behind her.

"I want to make movies, Mr. Scott."

"Just call me, Quinn. Everyone else does." He ignored the coffee and stared at her intensity. Her face was flushed, but her eyes had the determined look of a Valkerie. If she'd had a sword in her hand, he might have retreated.

"Do you think I like being a production assistant? Well, picking up your film at the airport every day is not what I went to film school for. I want to write, direct and produce, and while I'm willing to do whatever it takes to get there, you aren't cooperating."

Quinn folded his arms over his chest and concealed his amusement. He was enjoying her passion for her work, enjoying watching her find out that she could stand up to him and win respect. "*I'm* not cooperating?"

"Have you read my script?"

"I've been busy."

"If I wait until you're *not* busy, we'll both be dead."

"Maggie probably has the script in her file cabinet. Why don't you find it and give it to me?"

"Why?"

"Well, it probably isn't good for mopping up coffee. Maybe I'll read it," he suggested wryly.

Kimberly fisted her hands on her hips and raised her chin. "If you don't read it this month, I'm going to send it over to a friend of mine at ADM."

"That was your first mistake," he instructed kindly. "But you were doing really well until then."

"Huh?" Kimberly backed away, looking alarmed by her previous boldness.

"Lesson number one. After I told you I'd read the script, you got what you wanted. That's the time to shut up. Your threat went too far. It wasn't necessary and could have pissed me off, but it didn't this time— so take it easy, okay?"

"Sorry. I'm new at this."

"Hey, if you bring as much passion to your writing as you do to spilling my coffee, the script must be great."

Quinn glanced down at the messages he could no longer read. "Do you remember if anyone important called?"

"Laine Lamonde's agent. George Lucas and your father."

"Anyone who didn't leave their name?"

Kimberly looked at him and her eyes widened. "I got a strange call from some woman with a French accent. She wouldn't leave her name, but how did you know…"

"Did she leave a message?"

"Yeah. She said to make sure you watched your film at one o'clock sharp. Any idea who she is?"

"Not a clue." Which was the truth. And Quinn couldn't have been more pleased. "If anyone female shows up unannounced for an appointment while I'm watching the film, let her through. Don't look at her too closely. And don't ask questions or you might scare her away."

Kimberly scooted around his desk to mop up the spill. "Got it."

MAGGIE SLEPT IN LATE and woke up wonderfully refreshed. Then she set about what she did best—made plans for the day. After a wonderful massage and facial, she felt ready to call Kimberly and see how things were progressing at the office.

In the mall, Maggie stopped in front of a pile of on-sale lingerie and dialed her cell phone.

Kimberly answered on the first ring. ''Mr. Scott's office, Kimberly speaking.''

''How's it going?''

''Where are you?''

''Shopping for panties. Tell me why do thongs cost the most when they have the least amount of material?''

Kimberly ignored the rhetorical question. ''He's going to read my script.''

''Atta girl. What did you do? Knock him over the head with it?''

Kimberly laughed happily. ''Actually I spilled coffee all over his messages and yelled at him.''

''Quite a technique.''

''I think he's in an especially good mood because he expects a nameless woman to show up while he's watching that film in the dark.''

''That's what I want him to think. I'm sure by now he suspects that I work for him but since thousands of people work here, I'm still safe. And I'm not showing up yet.''

''Why not?''

''Because I want him anxious to see me.''

''If you ask me, he's already there.''

''And I want security to see me come into the

building. The day and night shifts change at five. I plan to enter at ten to five. If you can, before you leave, mention to Quinn that I dropped by to pick up my spare set of keys. Tomorrow I'll claim that I locked mine in the car while at the doctor's.''

"If Quinn checks with security, you'll be right where you said you'd be.''

"Exactly.''

"But if you don't come when the room is dark, he's going to see your face.''

"I've got it covered. There's a package coming at four. Make sure he opens it.''

"Okay.''

"Thanks, Kimberly.''

"I should be thanking you for giving me the chance to fill in today. I'd never have worked up the nerve to yell at him if I hadn't been so close to tears.''

"He's going to love your script. I know it.''

Maggie hung up the phone, brought her purchases to the counter and signed the credit card receipt without looking at the total. She hurried out of the store, wondering exactly what Quinn would do when her package arrived. She sensed that after their first night together, he'd been determined to discover Maggie's identity, but after their phone sex, he'd seemed more willing to go along with her scheming. And since he knew he would be with her again, no doubt he figured he had plenty of time to learn her name. In the meantime, he should enjoy the tryst she had planned. She just hoped his curiosity wouldn't get the best of him.

Because she trusted Quinn to keep his word, she'd agreed to this meeting today. And if she was risking her job, so be it. Sometimes a girl had to do what a girl had to do. If she backed off now, she'd regret the decision for the rest of her life. She had too much emotionally invested in seeing this through to hold back. If Quinn fired her...there were other jobs.

She imagined Quinn opening the box she'd messengered over. He would find the gift inside that she'd promised. And instructions.

She could hardly wait, as anticipation energized her nerves until she could barely swallow any of her lunch salad. Would Quinn be wearing her gift?

QUINN WATCHED THE MOVIE, expecting his lover to slip into the dark room at any time. He'd already decided that he would turn off the movie as soon as she entered, giving her the darkness she needed to preserve her identity. When she didn't arrive, disappointment washed over him. Perhaps she hadn't been able to sneak past security. He didn't want to consider that she might go back on her word and not show at all.

Quinn's obsession with his mystery woman had intensified, and he thought he knew why. Besides the sizzling sex, she had yet to reveal her identity. Or what she wanted. He suspected as soon as she did, his obsession would end and she would be just another woman who wanted to act in his films. However, in the meantime, he'd be a fool to end the excitement. He hadn't ever looked forward to seeing a woman as much as he did her.

After viewing the film, he'd spent the afternoon fielding phone calls with agents, financiers and writers, which didn't improve his temper. Where was she?

Why hadn't she come to him? Or at least phoned to let him know that she would be in touch.

"Quinn, I just signed for a package for you," Kimberly told him. "There's no return address."

No address? It might be from *her*. "Please bring it to me."

"I've another stack of messages, too." Kimberly placed the messages on his desk next to the brown box. She'd actually managed to enter and exit his office with only a minor stumble.

"Thanks." He waited until she'd closed the door behind her before reaching for the box, but when his private phone rang, he picked up the phone instead. This red line came directly into his office and didn't go through his secretary. Only the most important people in his life had the number. His parents. A few close friends. And the men who financed his films.

Quinn could have opened the box and answered his phone at the same time, but both things were important to him, each requiring his full attention.

Caller ID told him Derek Parker was on the other end of the line. "Yes, Derek, what can I do for you today?"

"I've heard some rumors that I don't like," Derek told him bluntly.

"Oh?"

"Yeah. Laine's in Vancouver."

She was? Her agent, Tyrol, had told Maggie that she was heading out to this coast. Had Tyrol been deliberately vague to mislead him? Quinn hadn't gotten to his position in life by making assumptions. And he knew Derek well enough to know that the man had checked out the rumor before calling him. He was just grateful the appearance of the fake Laine at Hotel Vendaz hadn't made the tabloids or he might have had even more of a mess on his hands.

"I have a meeting with Laine's agent next week," Quinn responded.

"Dan O'Donnel's in Vancouver."

"I see."

"Whoever signs her is getting my full backing. Your film is better, but whoever signs Laine will have a huge hit."

Quinn appreciated the other man's honesty. His film would still be made with or without Laine, but he needed a huge budget to pull off the period piece and authentic sets he had in mind. Without the funding, his film wouldn't do well at the box office.

He needed to find Laine and sign her before O'Donnel did. He only hoped he wasn't already too late. "Thanks for the information. I think maybe a trip to Vancouver this weekend might be in order."

"Take the company jet."

Quinn checked his PDA and made a note to himself to have Maggie cancel several appointments. "How about golf next week?"

"Monday morning?"

"Sounds good."

"Quinn, there's one more thing."

"Yes?"

"I heard Laine Lamonde is quite the man-eater. Watch your balls when dealing with her."

Quinn's pulse quickened. He enjoyed nothing more than a good challenge. And now that Derek had called his attention to Laine, Quinn wondered whether her plane trouble and her delayed trip had been deliberate. Maybe her appearance at the Hotel Vendaz had made the French papers and she was miffed at being upstaged by an impersonator.

Another less experienced man might have been more concerned about O'Donnel's bid to sign Laine, but Quinn suspected the lady was simply trying to up her price. Interesting—and melodramatic, but then actresses loved melodrama. But he would deal with Laine later.

Right now his fingers itched to open his present and he reached for the box. Inside, he found a black silk blindfold and a note. His heartbeat quickened as he picked up the white piece of paper scented with jasmine. Words had been cut from a magazine and newspaper then glued to make a message.

Dear Quinn,

I will come to you very soon in your office. Please be ready for me by wearing the blindfold. And only the blindfold. If your door is shut, I will assume you are inside, waiting for me, naked.

Quinn grinned at her audacity. The idea was kinky, kooky and kindled a heat in his groin that made up his mind for him. This time she wanted to be in control and he had more than enough backbone to let her.

Quinn buzzed his production assistant. ''Kimberly?''

''Yes, sir.''

''The woman who I spoke to you about earlier is going to pay me a visit.''

''The one without a name?''

"Yeah."

"Can you stay until she arrives and then lock the door behind you?"

"Sure."

"And absolutely no one but her is to come into my office."

"Sir?"

"Yes."

"How do I know that I'm letting the right person through?" Quinn supposed Kimberly's question was reasonable and he really didn't have an answer, but that was part of the fun.

He thought it over and finally answered. "I'm not expecting anyone else."

"Okay. Maggie locked her keys in her car and she just stopped by to get her spare set. She said to tell you that she'll be in tomorrow."

"Thanks."

Quinn closed the blackout drapes and then the blinds, enveloping his office in privacy from the outside world. He turned out the lights and then removed all of his clothes. The room was dark, but light filtered in from under the door, enough for him to find the blindfold and tie it over his eyes.

With the last bit of light gone, he couldn't see at all. His leather chair felt cool against his bare skin. He felt around his desk and picked up the note, sniffed again. The scent of jasmine reassured him that a real woman was going to show up.

However, he realized that even with the door unlocked, it was unlikely that the unthinkable would happen and the wrong person would accidentally walk into his office to find him sitting there naked. Blindfolded. How awkward would that be? But people didn't barge into his office. Never. They knocked.

In any other place in the world, a man found in his position might lose his standing by exhibiting such behavior—but this was California. As long as two adults were willing and over the age of consent, no one cared what they did in their private time.

And no one from Simitar Studios would dare enter his office with Kimberly guarding the door. If Maggie had been in, she might knock, then barge in, but she was off sick. He really wasn't risking that much. And Quinn had the uncanny knack of following his gut, of being a maverick, and having things work out for him. Even if someone entered, the room was dark, and he was hidden behind the desk from the waist down.

So why was he listening to every creak and groan? Why were the hairs on his arms standing on end? And why had all his blood gone directly south?

She wasn't even here. He was all alone. Waiting for her. And every minute seemed like an hour.

8

MAGGIE WALKED INTO SIMITAR Studios and nodded
hello to the security guard. She held a tissue to her
nose as if she needed it. But she was far from feeling
sick. Every step she took in her new thong panties
reminded her where she was going and why.

Her stomach clenched at the thought of a naked,
blindfolded Quinn waiting for her in his office. Would
he follow her instructions?

She had her plan worked out. By now Kimberly
should have told him Maggie had come and gone. If
she entered his office and found him dressed, she
would be his secretary Maggie returning to pick up
some paperwork she'd forgotten and to assure her
boss she would be back at work tomorrow. If he was
blindfolded and naked, she would be his lover.

However, every plan had inherent risks and while
confidence bloomed in her gut, she couldn't be positive she had every angle covered. That's where she
should be scared, but instead exhilaration simmered
in her blood. Each step she took, she had to refrain
from bouncing in excitement.

She took the elevator up to his office, her palms
damp with the fear of discovery, her heartbeat racing
with her need to be with Quinn again. To go with her

panties, she'd purchased a new push-up bra that left her nipples bared to rub against the silky material of her blouse. Maggie wore a sweater over her blouse to hide her erect nipples from the casual glances of her fellow workers. Her skirt brushed against her bare legs as she strode quickly down the hallway filled with people leaving work and exiting the building.

She nodded to acquaintances, her stomach fluttering with nerves as she passed through a long hallway and several private offices before reaching her own. Kimberly was sitting behind her desk, frowning over a stack of messages, but looked up the moment Maggie entered.

Maggie put her finger to her lips, a silent reminder to Kimberly not to speak. She didn't want to give Quinn a clue that she was there—not until she walked through his door.

Kimberly shot her a thumbs-up signal, glanced at the clock, picked up her purse and left the outer office, locking the door behind her with a click that caused Maggie's nerves to shimmy down her spine. In the three years she'd worked for Quinn, she'd never been locked in the office alone with him.

She took a deep breath and let it out slowly.

Now all she had to do was figure out if she was going to act as Quinn's secretary or his lover. Her tummy clenched, her nipples hardened in anticipation and her new panties were already damp. All reactions Quinn would know nothing about—unless he'd followed her instructions.

Maggie placed her hand on the doorknob. Nerves warred with excitement.

Her plan would work, but what if Quinn went along with her instructions, waited until she was in a compromising position—and then removed his blindfold? *Oh, God.* Though she'd tried her best to think of every contingency, she could slip up on a little detail that might give her away. She'd switched toothpaste and deodorant brands, avoided her usual hair gel and scent. Could she have forgotten anything that might give her away?

More important, did she trust him to follow her rules? Walking through the door could ruin everything—but probably not. She reminded herself that he hadn't removed her mask the first night she'd made love to him.

But he'd had no reason to. Then, he'd believed he was with Laine. Then, he'd believed he knew his lover's name.

By now, Quinn had to be burning with curiosity. She'd have to make it very clear to him that they couldn't be together unless he agreed to remain blindfolded.

But, again, she would have to rely on Quinn keeping his word.

Logic told her that Quinn's word was as good as a signature on a contract. He was first and foremost a businessman. And unlike many people in the film world, Quinn's word was his bond. Her fingers tightened, then loosened on the doorknob. Quinn hadn't yet promised her anything.

Walking through that door might be risking her job. However Quinn's admission to his secretary that he was interested in his lover beyond what they shared sexually had egged her on. Quinn had been intrigued that she hadn't asked him a favor, that she wanted him simply because she was in lust.

She had to admit that the excitement of her secret added an extra zing. But they already shared so much more than fantastic sex. They worked well together. She suspected they could also be best friends, if the employee-employer scenario could be overcome. And she was learning that they also shared a similar risk-taking persona. Perhaps Quinn's famous ability to gamble on an unknown director or actress appealed to her on levels she hadn't known existed inside herself. But now that she'd found the courage to act out her secret fantasies, no way could she stop. She liked the new, bold Maggie too much to end things with Quinn. So if she lost her job, then so be it. She understood the danger. She'd minimized the risk.

She licked her bottom lip. Imagined Quinn waiting on the other side of the door.

Was he thinking about her?

Wondering if she'd show?

Was he already hard with excitement?

If she walked away, she'd never know what she would have missed.

Open the door.

Maggie ordered her fingers to turn the knob. The room was dark. Maggie pushed the light switch and set the dimmer to low.

Quinn sat at his desk. Blindfolded, shirtless. He must have heard her flick on the lights, but he didn't say a word. Just waited for her to speak as if he expected her demand.

Using her French accent, she spoke in a husky tone. "If you want me to stay, you must promise not to remove the blindfold until after I'm gone."

"Agreed."

Quinn had no problem with her demand. In fact, he was beginning to realize that not knowing anything about the woman lent a definite edge of excitement to their encounters. He had every guy's fantasy in real life, a sexy woman and no commitments or responsibilities—none.

He could put up with his burning curiosity and the mystery of her real identity in exchange for more moments like this one. The precise click of her heels approaching across his marble floor had his body tensing in anticipation. And he wondered what she'd do first. Kiss him? Go down on him?

She walked behind him, the scent of her light perfume, citrus maybe, teasing him. He ached to reach out and tug her into his arms, dip his head into her mass of hair and inhale a lungful of her heady fragrance. But sensing she wished him to remain compliant, stayed still.

For now.

The chair with him in it slid from behind his desk. "Ah, you have a beautiful body. All those hard muscles, just waiting for my touch."

"Is there anything you'd like me to do?" he asked in a conversational tone, but he was feeling anything but conversational. Sitting there blindfolded and naked, talking to his mystery lover and anticipating her next move had him wired for action. Every muscle in his arms and legs was tensed, ready. So sitting still and doing nothing took a lot of energy—which all poured into one very hard erection.

"I'm enjoying the view very much."

"Why don't you get more comfortable? Perhaps take off your blouse."

"Whatever you wish."

The slight rustle of her movements wasn't enough. He ached to touch her, but imagining what she was doing turned him on nearly as much. Would she boldly unfasten her blouse in a rush or take her time, allowing her fingers to linger? "Tell me what you are doing," he demanded.

"I'm unbuttoning my blouse. The top button is sticking just a little and my fingers grazed my throat. Right here." She touched his throat with just a fingertip and, in surprise, he almost jumped out of his skin.

She'd left a waft of scent behind. Not citrus. Jasmine. Like the note she'd sent earlier. She'd also left him with the impression that she was standing close enough that if he reached out his hand, he could skim his fingers over her warm flesh.

"Have you started on the second button yet?" he asked.

"Oh, yes. This one is just above the hollow of my breasts. About here."

Tease. He was prepared for her to touch him again. First, strands of her hair grazed his shoulder, which should have warned him. But when her sharp teeth nipped him, then licked away the smarting, he had to clench the arms of his chair to prevent himself from yanking her into his arms and claiming her mouth.

"My oh my, aren't you tense."

He breathed in a ragged breath through his nose and released the air through his mouth in an attempt to calm his agitated nerves. Despite her words, she sounded quite pleased with his reaction.

She touched his inner thigh. "Ah, you are just the way I like a man. Tense and hard."

Yeah, she was definitely pleased that his sex was standing up for her. No woman had ever taken the time to play these kinds of games with him. He found the attention flattering and exciting and addictive. Oh, yeah. He could definitely get used to this kind of sex play.

"It's time to give the third button some attention," he told her, his voice husky.

"Yes, but I'm distracted. I went out this morning and bought a new dark green bra with panties to match. Too bad you can't see me."

"Describe yourself."

"The bra curves under my breasts and lifts me up, creating a very deep cleavage, just like I pushed up my breasts while I played with them during our phone conversation. I'll bet you'd like to use your hands to lift my breasts like this."

He clenched his teeth to prevent himself from doing just that. Her voice, so softly provocative, and her words, full of imagery that left his imagination working overtime, had him ready to sweep everything off his desk, wrap his hands around her waist and have her right on his desk.

Live the emotion™
Anytime. Anywhere.
send for your 2 FREE ROMANCE BOOKS!
See Details Inside...

We'd like to send you 2 FREE BOOKS
and a surprise gift to introduce you to Harlequin®
Blaze™. Accept our special offer today and
Live the emotion™

HOW TO QUALIFY:

1. With a coin, carefully scratch off the silver area on the card at right to see what we have for you—**2 FREE BOOKS** and a **FREE GIFT**—ALL YOURS! **ALL FREE!**

2. Send back the card and you'll receive two brand-new Harlequin® Blaze™ novels. These books have a cover price of $4.50 each in the U.S. and $5.25 each in Canada, but they are yours to keep absolutely free!

3. There's no catch. You're under no obligation to buy anything. We charge nothing—ZERO—for your first shipment and you don't have to make any minimum number of purchases—not even one!

4. The fact is, thousands of readers enjoy receiving books by mail from the Harlequin Reader Service® Program. They enjoy the convenience of home delivery…they like getting the best new novels at discount prices, BEFORE they're available in stores…and they love their *Heart to Heart* subscriber newsletter featuring author news, horoscopes, recipes, book reviews and much more!

5. We hope that after receiving your free books you'll want to remain a subscriber. But the choice is yours—to continue or cancel, any time at all. So why not take us up on our invitation with no risk of any kind. You'll be glad you did!

GET A *Free* MYSTERY GIFT…

We can't tell you what it is…but we're sure you'll like it! A FREE gift just for giving the Harlequin Reader Service® Program a try!

Visit us online at
www.eHarlequin.com

Your FREE Gifts include:

- 2 Harlequin® Blaze™ books!
- An exciting mystery gift!

HARLEQUIN®
Live the emotion™

Scratch off
the silver area to see what the
Harlequin Reader Service®
Program has for you.

YES! I have scratched off the silver area above. Please send
me the **2 FREE BOOKS** and gift for which I qualify.
I understand I am under no obligation to purchase any
books, as explained on the back and on the opposite page.

350 HDL DU4G   150 HDL DU4W

FIRST NAME   LAST NAME

ADDRESS

APT #   CITY

STATE/PROV.   ZIP/POSTAL CODE

(H-B-07/03)

THE HARLEQUIN READER SERVICE® PROGRAM—Here's how it works:

Accepting your 2 free books and mystery gift places you under no obligation to buy anything. You may keep the books and gift and return the shipping statement marked "cancel." If you do not cancel, about a month later we'll send you 4 additional books and bill you just $3.80 each in the U.S., or $4.21 each in Canada, plus 25¢ shipping and handling per book and applicable taxes if any.* That's the complete price and — compared to cover prices of $4.50 in the U.S. and $5.25 in Canada — it's quite a bargain! You may cancel at any time, but if you choose to continue, every month we'll send you 4 more books, which you may either purchase at the discount price or return to us and cancel your subscription.

*Terms and prices subject to change without notice. Sales tax applicable in N.Y. Canadian residents will be charged applicable provincial taxes and GST.

"Ah, perhaps your silence means that I'm not holding your attention." Like he wouldn't recall every single word. "But there's something else about my new lingerie that might interest you even more." She paused and he concentrated on digging his fingers into the chair's arms in order to keep himself seated.

"What?" he growled.

She chuckled as if she knew exactly how she'd fired him into a blaze of need, despite not having yet touched him. He needed to slow down, but he didn't know how, not with the way she kept fanning his fire.

"This lovely bra doesn't cover much of my breasts. I can clearly see my nipples."

The image she painted with her words made him ache to see her again. Instead he had to rely on the memory of their first night together. She'd had lovely round breasts, full and high. The dusky pink areolas had shown off her tight little nipples and he clenched his fingers into the chair to prevent himself from reaching out to touch them.

"Are your nipples all pointy and hard right now?"

"What do you think?" She brushed the tip of her breast along his lips, but before he could capture the tempting bud and draw it into his mouth, she pulled away.

His temperature heated until beads of sweat popped out on his neck. "You are a tease."

"And you are enjoying me, yes?"

"I'll enjoy you more when we touch."

With no warning, she captured the head of his sex in her mouth, ran her tongue over the lip. He gasped in surprise at the sudden heat. Just as suddenly as she'd surrounded him in warmth, she pulled back to leave the cool air dancing on his moist skin.

"I will touch you where and when and how I please," she told him. "But right now, this dang blouse is in my way." *Dang?* She'd pretty much given up on the phony French accent. "I'm unbuttoning the last two buttons and taking off my shirt."

He envisioned her wearing that sexy bra. Her firm high breasts lightly tanned, her pink nipples taut against the dark green—like a Christmas present waiting to be unwrapped. He hadn't known that his erection could harden more, but even his balls had rolled up tight, straining to reach her. But instead of her warm, welcoming heat, his flesh met the vacuum of lonely space.

He could hear the rustle of material as she did something to her blouse, the click of her high heels as she returned to him. "Are you enjoying my little striptease?"

"It'll be one of my all-time favorite memories, I'm sure," he told her wryly—but he meant it.

"Are you going to have trouble staying in that chair while I remove my skirt?"

What a question! He swallowed a knot of desire. He didn't want to refuse her anything. However he wasn't sure he could do as she asked. And he didn't want to lie, either. He chewed his bottom lip, uncharacteristically undecided.

"Well?"

"The mind is willing, but the flesh has other ideas."

"I came prepared for such an eventuality."

Interesting. "You did?" She fascinated him on so many levels. Not many women would have created a scenario like this one, even fewer would have admitted to making preparations—for that meant that the lady was willing to make the first moves, even accept rejection. And she didn't mind his knowing that she thought him worth making preparations for.

She had a way of almost reaching into his inner psyche and giving him what he needed. She seemed to know him better than he knew himself.

"What do you think about my tying your wrists to the chair's arms? And your ankles to the legs?"

"You want me at your mercy?"

"You already are. You just haven't yet admitted the obvious to yourself."

He tested her. "What if I say no?"

"What if I leave now?" she countered.

"Do it." He spit the words out like an order before he thought too hard or too long. He was going with his gut instincts here, guts that were raw with excitement. But trusting a woman whose name he didn't even know might be the biggest mistake he'd ever made.

"Don't move."

He felt her tying a piece of ribbon around first one wrist and then the other, very fine ribbon, ribbon that he could break with ease if he chose. And that's when he realized that the ribbon was symbolic. She was using his own wants, needs and desires to tie him.

When she finished, she kissed his lips, then trailed more kisses along his jaw. While her mouth teased and taunted with tenderness, she boldly cupped his balls, squeezed lightly as his sex jerked, then, like before, she pulled away. Her mixture of sweet and audacious made her unpredictable and incredibly erotic. He heard her zipper coming down and demanded, "Tell me how you look."

"My panties are green, brief, very brief. In fact, they are a thong." He sucked in air at the image. "And I didn't have to worry about my bikini line since yesterday I shaved almost everywhere."

He needed to see her. Touch her. His mouth went dry as he forced himself to sit still. And even then, he couldn't resist torturing himself by asking, "How do the panties feel?"

"Naughty. Tight. Damp. I'm bending over to slip off my skirt."

"Come here so I can touch you."

The click of her heels told him she was coming near. "Turn your palm up."

Since she'd tied the ribbon loosely, he could turn his hand over without breaking the ribbon. She leaned over him and her lips brushed his. At the same time, his fingers slid over her lace panties, edging over flesh that was as smooth as satin.

Oh so sensitive, she jerked at his first touch. Her head bumped his and his blindfold slid up. For one split second before the blindfold slid back down to cover his eyes again, he saw his mystery lover's face.

Maggie!

IF MAGGIE HADN'T IMMEDIATELY thrust her tongue into his mouth, he might have said her name aloud.

Maggie was his secret lover.

Maggie was seducing him. It was Maggie who had taken Laine's place. Maggie with whom he'd had phone sex. Maggie who had him naked and blindfolded and tied with ribbons to his office chair.

And she had no idea what had just happened. No idea that the blindfold had slipped. His thoughts whirled crazily in his head. No wonder she knew him so well. No wonder she could plan around his schedule.

So how come he'd never known that Maggie could kiss like his hottest fantasy? How come he hadn't known that beneath her businesslike clothes was a woman with the curves of a goddess? He was so stunned, it was moments before he realized that she was no longer kissing him. The knowledge may have stunned him but it certainly hadn't diminished his desire for her.

Sweet, bold, sexy Maggie. He wanted her just as much now as when she'd been his mystery woman. Maggie who never asked him for anything for himself. Maggie who kept his chaotic life sane. Maggie who was the best lover he'd ever had.

"I'm sliding my panties over my hips."

He could say her name and end their games, but he wasn't crazy. Why should he stop when every nerve in him screamed to drive into her heat? When his every cell craved her touch? When his soul begged for more?

He still couldn't quite believe that his secretary's clever fingers were unrolling a condom over him. When she finally straddled him, captured him in her heat, and rode him, taking him higher and higher, he could barely think of anything but the pleasure.

Pleasure from Maggie.

It was Maggie's tight little nipples grazing his chest. Maggie's lips on his. Maggie sheathing him, riding him. Urging him on with soft little moans in the back of her throat until the blood roared in his ears and his body gave himself up to her. And just when he was about to orgasm, it was Maggie who pulled away. Maggie who left him reeling. Maggie who pressed her fingers to the base of his erection to stop him from coming.

"Not yet," she told him, her jasmine scent driving him as wild as her sweet little nips to his ear and her bold grip on his sex. "I'm going to cool you down and then heat you up all over again."

Leaving his mind reeling and his flesh slick with sweat, she walked to his office bar. He heard her open the fridge, then close the door. A moment later she returned and there was the sound of a cap being twisted off. Then she was trickling drops of cool water all over him, then lapping it off his hot skin with her neat and ingenious tongue.

His body cooled and surged back twice as hard. His fingers were back to clenching the chair's arms. Her teeth were nipping his neck. Her fingers tweaking his nipples. And then she straddled him, once again taking him inside her sweet heat.

He tried to hold back, wait. But all too soon he was tensing and about to come. When she pulled away this time, and again stopped his orgasm from erupting, he had to bite back a shout.

"You can wait just a little longer, can't you, babe?"

"Yeah." But he couldn't have. Not without her little trick of applying pressure to the base of his sex. She had taken total control of him, even dictating the moment when he'd orgasm. And he'd never felt sexier. Never felt more in need of a woman.

"I'm going to cool you off with an ice cube. Think you can take it like a man?"

She didn't wait for him to answer. The cold on his balls as she moved the cube over him created a fiery sensation. He didn't understand how cold could feel hot. He didn't understand why he was having sex with his secretary. And he didn't understand why he felt as though the top of his head was about to blow off. he only knew that if he didn't get release soon, he would be reduced to begging.

The ice cube was melting way too slowly. He gritted his teeth, determined not to say a word.

And then she took him inside her again. She rode him and he urged her on with his kiss and his words. "Come with me. Come with me now."

And she spasmed around him. The heat and the cold drove him wild. Her nipples grazed his chest and with her mouth on his, she had him spiraling, exploding. Careening out of control.

When he could once more think, he realized that his wrists had broken the ribbons and his arms had come around her, cradling her against his chest. He held her tenderly for a long time until their breathing slowed and their blood cooled.

And he didn't want to think that he was holding

dear bold and reckless Maggie. Right now, after the most fantastic sex of his life, he just wanted to revel in how good he felt, not in his strong feelings of happiness. Later would be soon enough to decide what to do.

QUINN LET MAGGIE WALK OUT the door without telling her what he knew. He'd been in business too long to show his cards before he decided whether to hold, call or fold. He couldn't recall the last time a woman had so shaken him and intrigued him. No wonder he couldn't keep a coherent thought in his head.

Quinn had three-and-a-half hours before he had to meet Dan for drinks. Enough time to drive to Malibu for some father-son advice. Most men would consider talking to good-old dad about women a weakness, but most men didn't have Jason Scott for a father.

As a producer, when Quinn couldn't find the right face, he consulted the best casting agent in town. When he couldn't find the right subplot, he brought in a top-notch writer to help. When he needed terrific special effects, he went to a master. And when he couldn't figure out a woman, he went to an expert—his father.

Jason knew and understood women better than any man Quinn knew. Hell, he'd had decades of experience. But his father also hated to be pinned down in a serious discussion, so Quinn didn't call in advance.

The Pacific Ocean was flat this evening, the beach empty. Jason's contemporary mansion perched precariously on the cliff, a testament to human engineering and man's obsession with waterfront property. Although Jason had a home in Beverly Hills, a penthouse in New York and a town house in London, the fifteen-thousand-square-foot beach bungalow was his favorite of his father's properties.

Jason's butler greeted Quinn, and shortly thereafter he'd joined his father on the terrace. At Quinn's entrance, Jason shut the magazine he'd been reading, stood and hugged his son. "What brings you out here?"

"A woman."

Jason's eyebrows rose. "Who?"

"My secretary."

"Is she pregnant?"

"No."

"Cheating on you?"

"No."

"Selling secrets to the paparazzi?"

"No." At least he hoped not!

"Well then, what's the problem?" Jason settled back in his lounge chair, laced his hands behind his head and crossed his feet, creating the picture of relaxation. His handsome face soaked up the sun's rays, but not one brown spot marred his camera-perfect face. The man had one-in-a-billion genes that had made him a wealthy and popular star whose career had spanned decades and who attracted a myriad of women. If Quinn hadn't known him well, he would have thought his father wasn't concerned. But Quinn knew better. Despite the superb act he put on for the world, his father had a very good brain. However, showing his intelligence frightened directors, producers and could hamper his career. More important, au-

diences expected their stars to be like the boy next-
door. A little edgy, but sympathetic. High intellects
tended to turn people off. So his father had mastered
the role of "movie star."

"I don't know what Maggie wants," Quinn admitted. "She took Laine Lamonde's place at the masquerade ball. Used a French accent and didn't take
off the mask when we made love."

"And now she's holding that against you?"

Odd how his father kept suspecting the worst—just
like Quinn. Had he learned that cynicism at Jason's
knee? Or was it simply the way Hollywood worked?
You scratch my back, I'll scratch yours.

"She's not threatening me or asking for anything."

"And the problem is?" Jason prodded.

"I can't figure out her angle."

"Maybe she doesn't have one."

Quinn took a chair beside his father. "You believe
that?"

"No. But it does happen. Your mother loved me
before I was famous." Jason sounded sad, but philosophical.

One of the great mysteries of Quinn's life was the
reason for his parents' divorce. Neither of them would
speak of it. Yet there clearly remained a fondness
between them. He considered it a measure of their
maturity that neither of them had ever spoken badly
to him about the other.

When Quinn remained silent, his father actually
frowned at him, risking a wrinkle. "I can't give
advice without information. What haven't you
told me?"

"I'm not supposed to know that it was Maggie that I made love with."

"So why not just go on pretending that it never happened?"

"I guess I could...." Quinn saw no reason to give his father all the details. If his father wanted to assume they'd made love just once, it was okay by him because it didn't change his dilemma—what to do next.

Quinn knew he couldn't go along with his father's suggestion and pretend their lovemaking hadn't happened. But he didn't know why. Obviously Maggie had struck some chord in him. For the past few days, he'd felt as if he could walk on air. He hadn't slept much and he had twice his usual energy. Maggie had done that for him and he wasn't about to give her up, not as his secretary, not as his lover and not as the friend she was becoming.

So what if she distracted him? Hell, he'd spent more time thinking about Maggie than he had about signing Laine. Yet, Quinn always put work first, his personal life second. Maggie had turned his priorities upside down, and instead of resenting her, he wanted to kiss her. Damn it.

His father read Quinn's reluctance to say more with the ease of an actor who studied character for a living. "She was that unforgettable, huh?"

Quinn grunted his assent, worried how their working relationship might change. Maggie was the best assistant he'd ever had. He depended on her nose for business, her instinct for who was friend or foe. He didn't want to stop working with her any more than he wanted to give up making love to her.

"You could just come out and tell Maggie that you know that she's the one who took Laine's place."

Quinn snapped his fingers and grinned for the first time since he'd made his startling discovery that his feelings for Maggie were stronger than he'd ever suspected. "Or I could do a little one-upmanship."

"Sounds interesting. Care to elaborate?"

Quinn shook his head. He squeezed his father's shoulder with affection. "Thanks, Dad, you've been a great help."

MAGGIE CAME TO WORK THE NEXT morning with a light step, pleased that she'd turned her opportunity with Quinn into more than a one-time fling. What they had together, she couldn't exactly categorize. She certainly hadn't changed her mind about his suitability as a permanent partner. Quinn might respond to her, to something she saw in him, but he wasn't capable of love and stability and commitment. And even if he didn't react to the constant flow of beautiful young women throwing themselves at him, why would she want to deal with them? Maggie was too smart to set herself up for that kind of heartache. However, she could continue their sexual games—especially since Quinn didn't have a clue about her real identity.

When he called her into his office to dictate a fax, she couldn't help recalling that only yesterday Quinn had been sitting there naked and blindfolded and tied with her ribbons to his chair. At the memory, a delicious shimmy of heat coursed through her. But she kept her expression neutral and her eyes cast downward.

Maggie took out her pad and pen. "Who's the fax going to?"

"A…friend. In Vancouver."

Quinn wasn't usually hesitant or evasive. Since lots of industry people filmed in Vancouver, Maggie figured that maybe Quinn was simply thinking hard about composing the letter.

"Does this friend have a name?"

"This is personal. I should probably write the letter myself, but I thought it could use your light touch."

Quinn had a former girlfriend who lived in Vancouver. Her name was Mia. She'd married a boat captain two years ago, and until recently, they'd run a charter business just north of the border. Maggie had heard through the grapevine that Mia was now divorced and looking for work in film again. Maybe Quinn wanted to hire her, but he'd said this was personal. What could he be thinking?

"So how should I address the letter?"

"I'll take care of that part. Just double-check the Canadian number before you fax it, okay?"

"Sure."

Maggie waited, pen poised above her pad, for Quinn to begin his letter.

"The last few days have been the best of my life."

Maggie almost melted in a puddle of warm satisfaction. Perhaps Quinn had been in touch with his ex-girlfriend since her recent divorce, and this letter to her was a final goodbye since he was having such a good time with his new lover.

"The first night was…"

"Yes?" she prodded.

"The first night was hot enough to singe the sheets."

Sheets? Confusion flooded through Maggie, washing away her previous satisfaction. Was Quinn talking about a date with Mia where he'd made love in a bed? Or was he speaking metaphorically about Maggie and Quinn's night together?

"And I'd never imagined after speaking to you on the phone that I could dream such erotic dreams."

Damn him. Why couldn't he be more specific?

Quinn paused, leaned forward and peered at her notes upside down. "Got all that?"

No. "Yes."

Quinn often made leaps in logic, jumping from subject to subject. Usually she had no trouble following him. However, right now he seemed deliberately obtuse and if she hadn't known better, she would have thought that he was doing so on purpose—but that made no sense. Perhaps her dual identity was getting in the way.

"I especially enjoyed our little tête-à-tête in my office. The blindfold really turned me on."

Oh, my God. He *was* talking about her time with him. Only he thought his ex-girlfriend had been his lover—not her. Heat rose to her face and in order to have an explanation for her reaction, Maggie dropped her pen. She bent over to retrieve it, pleased it had rolled under his desk. She took her time searching the floor, hoping Quinn would attribute the red flush she couldn't control to her mad scramble.

Quinn came around the desk and helped her to her feet, amusement in his eyes. From his pocket, he gallantly handed her another pen.

"Thanks." She accepted the pen, careful not to let

their fingers touch. Being close enough to him to breathe in his male fragrance brought back all-too-vivid memories of being skin to skin with him. Her body immediately responded, her heart rate accelerated, her breasts swelled and dampness seeped between her thighs.

And he'd attributed their lovemaking to another woman. He thought he'd been with Mia.

Maggie's throat closed up in panic. She had no idea what to do. Or say. Damn, what a mess.

She'd been so careful to mislead him from her true identity that he now believed his lover was someone else. Maggie wanted to fall through the floor. Disappear. Crawl into a hole and never come out.

Instead she tossed her hair over her shoulder and smoothed her skirt, then resettled in her chair. "Sorry."

"Read the last line back to me, please."

"The blindfold really turned me on," she read back. Perhaps he'd think her red face was due to the nature of his dictation. "So, you've finally figured out who your mystery woman is, huh?"

"I believe so."

"Well, who is she?" Maggie demanded, her voice shaky, suspecting for a moment that he was playing with her, that he knew it had not been Mia, but Maggie who he'd made love to.

"I'd rather not say until I ask her first."

Oh my God. She was still safe. He didn't think she was his lover.

Quinn suddenly speared her with a fierce stare. "Have you ever made love blindfolded?"

Maggie's pulse raced. Quinn never asked his secretary personal questions, and for a moment she thought that he might be teasing her. Or on a fishing expedition to see if she would confess.

But when she shook her head, Quinn shot her a sheepish grin. "You might want to try it with a friend sometime."

Quinn spoke as matter-of-factly as if he were recommending a restaurant. He probably was thinking just how uncomfortable he'd made his conservative secretary and had tried to put her at ease. What he didn't know, couldn't guess, was that the idea turned her on so much that she had to press her thighs together tightly, afraid the dampness between her legs might go through her skirt.

Maggie regrouped quickly. Since Quinn seemed so open to discussing his love life with his secretary, she would take advantage of the situation. "Let me get this straight. A woman let you blindfold her?"

Quinn's brows raised. "Actually, she asked me to wear a blindfold."

"Oh."

"And now I want to reciprocate the favor."

"Hmm."

"So I have to fly to Vancouver. You do understand?"

What was to misunderstand? He wanted to make love to the woman who had turned him on. Only he thought that woman lived in Vancouver.

Way to go, Maggie. Way to screw up big time.

She supposed this was the moment she should confess, before Quinn tried to blindfold some poor woman who would have no idea what kind of game he was playing. Yet, Quinn would show Mia a very good time, and Maggie could barely contain her envy and resentment.

"Can you pack and be ready to leave by five o'clock?"

"You want me to go with you? I don't understand." That had to be the understatement of the century. She was almost back to thinking that he knew she was his lover, but then he dashed that idea into pieces.

"I'm taking the company jet. We can work on the way up and the way back."

Could this get any worse? He wanted her to go. So he could take the company jet and combine work and play. Executives did this all the time.

"Quinn, I'm just getting over my cold. It might hurt my ears to fly. Why don't you bring Kimberly?"

"She's too nosey. And too clumsy. Take a decongestant and you'll be fine. I promise, you'll be able to sleep late in the mornings because I want time alone with my woman."

"But—"

"Come on, Maggie." He pulled the blindfold out of his pocket and ran it over his palm. "I'm eager to tie this over her eyes. You don't want me to be disappointed, do you?"

9

MAGGIE DROVE HOME on automatic pilot, grateful she didn't get a ticket, cut anyone off or cause an accident. How could this be happening to her? How could such a good plan have gone so awry?

When she'd been a kid, the worst thing that had ever happened during one of her plans was that the weather had refused to cooperate during an outdoor party. The decorations had been drenched, but everyone had moved inside and had a great time. And she'd successfully thrown a surprise dinner for her parents' thirtieth wedding anniversary, planning the entire party while out of town and flying in for the weekend. Quinn often had her oversee a multitude of social get-togethers for his stars—from intimate dinners to thousand-dollars-a-head charity events. And never before had her plans gone so wrong. Quinn thought another woman was responsible for their intimate encounters and she had no idea what to do now. She had never anticipated this turn of events and that upset her.

She didn't like any of her choices. She could come clean and tell Quinn that she was his mystery lover or remain silent and watch him hook up with one former lover after another in his search for Maggie. Why couldn't Quinn leave well enough alone?

When Quinn learned Mia was not the women who'd impersonated Laine, what would he do? Renew his acquaintance with his Mia? The thought annoyed her. Why should another woman benefit from Maggie's scheme?

Maggie parked her car and hurried up the steps to her apartment. She had only an hour to pack. At least she'd recently done laundry. But what was she going to do about Quinn?

She crouched down on hands and knees to pull her luggage out from under the bed and tossed it on top of the mattress, and it bounced and toppled onto her foot. Maggie wanted to sit down and cry. Or have a long girl-to-girl phone conversation with her sister in Michigan. Or fly home and let her mother fuss over her. But she didn't have time. So, instead, she grabbed the case and placed it back on the bed, resigned to the fact that she had to pack for a weekend in Vancouver while Quinn renewed his ties with his ex-girlfriend.

It wasn't fair.

It was bad enough that Quinn attributed all their delicious sex to another woman, bad enough that Maggie couldn't claim the credit, but now Quinn was going to pursue the other woman. And bring Maggie along to work.

Maggie tossed lingerie into her bag. No, it wasn't fair. But then life wasn't fair.

She ripped clothes off their hangers and stuffed them into the bag. Tossed in shoes, skirts, blouses without much thought. Her attire didn't matter. Quinn was interested in his ex, not her.

She didn't know why she hadn't anticipated such a possibility. Quinn was unpredictable, always springing surprises on her as well as his co-workers. While Maggie had certainly hoped Quinn would never figure out her identity, she hadn't thought he would believe she was another woman. Never anticipated he'd think she was Mia.

The hell of it was she wanted the credit but didn't want to come clean. What a mess.

Maggie stormed into her bathroom. Toothbrush. Toothpaste. Deodorant. Razor. Mouthwash. Hairbrush. Cosmetic bag.

She had two choices. She could tell Quinn the truth and risk losing her job. Maybe he wouldn't fire her, but she wasn't sure she was ready to face his temper, one that he usually kept in check but that could be quite alarming.

Her second option was to remain silent and watch him go to another woman and risk losing him.

What was she thinking?

How could she lose him? Quinn had never been hers in the first place. He'd never wanted Maggie his secretary as his lover, only Maggie the bombshell. And after what they'd shared, it hurt that he'd never seen the woman who'd worked by his side in any other light than as a coworker.

Maggie tugged on the zipper. In her haste, she'd overstuffed her bag. Sitting on the case, she again tried to tug the zipper shut. That's when she heard the ripping sound. The bag couldn't just rip a little. Something that she could patch with duct tape. Oh, no, the bag had split from end to end.

In frustration, Maggie shoved the bag onto the floor and kicked it. Now what? She didn't have another suitcase.

Her bell rang. Damn. Quinn was stopping by to pick her up since her apartment was on the way to the airport. The bell rang again. She ought not to answer it. Maybe Quinn would just go without her and she'd have an entire weekend to think what to do.

Quinn pounded on her door. "Come on, Maggie. We have to go."

With the racket he was making, she'd be lucky if she didn't get evicted. With a sigh, she walked through her living area and opened the front door. Quinn stood there in slacks and a long-sleeved shirt, his hair combed, his face freshly shaved. After the fight with her suitcase, she felt disheveled

"What's wrong?"

"The zipper on my suitcase broke."

Quinn had never been to her apartment before and peered at her secondhand furniture as if he expected a spare suitcase to pop out of the stuffing. "I don't suppose you have another?"

"You'll have to go without me."

"Don't be silly. I need you. You can just buy what you need from the hotel shop."

"My credit card is maxed out," she lied.

"We'll expense it to the company."

"But—"

"Come on," Quinn grabbed her arm. "Be spontaneous for once in your life." His voice sounded mocking. Is that what he thought? That Maggie was a stick-in-the-mud and couldn't be spontaneous?

Showed what he knew. "Just lock the door and let's go."

Their driver didn't say a word when she walked up to the limo with just her makeup bag. He tipped his cap and opened the door for them. Maggie slid onto the leather seat with dread in her heart. She couldn't make herself look at Quinn, simply stared out the window, her heart a miserable bundle of nerves.

Quinn didn't seem to mind that she ignored him. He took the opportunity to return several phone calls. Maggie barely listened to him cajole an agent, sweet-talk an actress and demand that a writer bring in a project on time.

Her stomach churned with anxiety and indecision. If she let Quinn approach his ex, she only had herself to blame. By the time the limo dropped them off at the private airstrip, and they entered the corporate jet, Maggie was no closer to a decision.

And as if Quinn was eager to get work out of the way and keep the rest of his weekend free, he kept her busy typing, all the way to Vancouver. Tired, grumpy, hungry and frazzled, she wanted a shower and room service, then a nap. But of course, the way her day was going, none of that happened.

Quinn insisted she peruse the hotel shops and buy what she needed first. Shopping with Quinn was quite the experience. When she looked at two dresses, try-ing to decide between them, he insisted she buy both. Then he told the salesclerk to add accessories and shoes.

"We can't charge all of this to Simitar Studios," Maggie told him.

"Would you stop worrying? Did you forget that my entertainment budget is practically limitless?" Quinn could probably see by her expression that she was about to argue. "Look, you're tired. Why don't you go up to the room and rest while I take care of the bill?"

"Fine." Maggie pressed the elevator button, unappreciative of the crisp Canadian air. She didn't expect to see Quinn again until Sunday when they left. By not making a decision, by choosing not to tell him the truth, she'd lost her opportunity.

But what else could she do?

Perhaps it was time to face the truth. She didn't want to give him up. Didn't want to lose him to another woman. Why couldn't they just continue their fling? Had that been asking for so much? She hadn't anticipated these kinds of complications and now she'd boxed herself into a corner.

Damn.

What was she going to do?

She didn't like her options. And as much as she wanted to blame Quinn for this latest twist in her scheme, she couldn't when the man didn't even know he'd been making love to Maggie and not Mia. Still…she'd thought what she and Quinn had together was so precious that his mistaking another woman for her hurt.

Had Quinn and Mia shared this kind of excitement in bed? Maggie sighed. She didn't want to go there. And yet, how could she not?

She unlocked her room and decided she wouldn't spend the weekend pouting. Vancouver had a reputation as a beautiful city and she'd never been here before. She'd fill every minute seeing the sights, eating in cheap restaurants so there'd be no chance of accidentally running into Quinn and Mia, and making sure that she didn't give herself time to feel sorry for herself.

Maggie kicked off her travel-grungy clothes and headed straight to the shower. She availed herself of the complimentary shampoo and conditioner and, afterward, the terry-cloth robe. She hoped her new clothes would arrive soon. In the meantime, she ordered room service.

She flicked on the television, but nothing caught her eye. And her thoughts kept returning to Quinn. What was he doing now? Where did he plan to spend his evening? And with whom?

She turned off the television with a sigh.

Maybe she should have just told him the truth. So what if he fired her? She could find another job. She really shouldn't have allowed their game to go so far, but she'd gotten carried away. Now all she had to look forward to was a weekend in a strange city. By her lonesome.

When Maggie heard the polite knock, she scrambled to open the door. Her new clothes had arrived in an assortment of bags. She couldn't remember buying quite so many things, but then she hadn't paid much attention as she'd been preoccupied with her dilemma.

"Thanks." She tipped the bellhop.

"Oh, yes, almost forgot. You're supposed to open this package first."

Maggie took the flat box from him. Before she could ask a question, he'd disappeared.

She sat on the bed and looked at the card attached to the box. Quinn had probably left her some final work to do.

Maggie opened the note. "Pick you up in thirty minutes. Please wear this."

Puzzled, Maggie opened the box. And found the blindfold.

God!

Quinn knew that Maggie was his secret lover. *He knew.*

And the entire trip up here he'd let her stew about thinking that he was coming to see another woman. Maggie wanted to scream. And she wanted to laugh. And dance.

She wanted to kiss him and shake him and yell at him all at the same time.

Quinn knew she was his lover. And he still wanted her.

If Quinn wanted her to wear the blindfold, he didn't intend to fire her. And he wanted to keep playing their games or he never would have brought her with him to Vancouver.

Relief and happiness made her eyes mist. Quinn knew. And he didn't care that his lover had turned out to be his secretary. He knew. And he wanted her. She'd never expected this turn of events. Never dared to hope. And suddenly all the aggravations of her day disappeared in a flash.

She wondered when he'd found out her secret and how. Then decided it didn't matter.

She only had twenty minutes left. Twenty minutes to get ready.

The realization that he'd planned for them to spend the entire weekend together in Vancouver had her skipping across the room. She was happy that he knew, delighted that he didn't mind that Maggie had deceived him.

Quinn had gone to a lot of trouble for her which meant that he was enjoying their time together as much as she'd hoped and suspected.

Where would Quinn take her blindfolded? Obviously he'd made elaborate plans. Hurriedly Maggie dressed. And realized they'd neglected to buy underwear. Since her old ones didn't appeal to her, she simply didn't wear any and the cool air under her skirt made her feel decidedly wicked. And after she donned the blindfold, she trembled in anticipation.

Obviously he intended to continue their fling.

QUINN OPENED MAGGIE'S DOOR at exactly seven o'clock. She was sitting in a chair fully dressed. She wasn't wearing the blindfold but running it between her fingers. And if that action wasn't enough to signal that something was wrong, her face, carefully blank, would have. The determined part of his character made him step inside and pull the door closed behind him with a soft click.

"Maggie. You okay?"

She wet her lip, a little nervously, perhaps. "When did you figure out…"

"That you were my lover?"

"Uh-huh."

She appeared more nervous than he would have imagined. However, before the evening was done, he wanted her comfortably snuggling against him. However, she appeared to need to talk things through first, and he supposed they'd waited long enough to have this intimate conversation.

Quinn kept his tone light. "The blindfold slipped for a second."

She folded her hands on her lap, but he noticed that her hands were trembling. Her voice, however, remained strong and husky. "And what did you think when you learned it was me?"

"That I was a very lucky man."

He strode close to her, bent down and kissed her lips. "By the way, I like your new hairstyle. It looks good on you." She jerked a little in surprise, then pulled back, her eyes wide and haunted looking. He took her icy fingers in his and smoothed his thumb over her out-of-control pulse at her wrist.

"And that fax you had me type was a setup? You let me think you were coming up here to be with another woman."

"I was hoping that fax would make you realize you could come to me, tell me the truth. When were you going to tell me it was you?"

"Why would I admit the truth when I thought you were coming to see another woman?" she countered.

He supposed she had a point. "Actually, I *am* up here to see another woman."

"What?"

He wished they could have the weekend to themselves, but he had to take care of business. "Laine's here in Vancouver and O'Donnel's trying to sign her to star in his film. I'm here to talk to her—"

"Fine."

Surely she couldn't be so withdrawn because he'd let her think that the meeting with another woman was an ex-girlfriend? Maggie wasn't petty and she'd deceived him, too. He didn't get it. She couldn't be angry about Laine. She knew how important the woman was to his career.

Maggie tried to pull her hand from his, but Quinn didn't let go. "Laine is having lunch with us tomorrow. Tonight is all ours. Now tell me what's wrong."

Maggie shook her head. "Exactly why did you bring me to Vancouver?"

Uh-oh. "So we could be together." He could have said more, but started out slowly.

"I've worked for you for four years. You never wanted us to be together before."

"We never made love before."

That statement earned him a scowl. "You never saw me as a potential lover, did you?"

Quinn sat next to Maggie on the bed. Despite the wintry edge in her tone, he still didn't release her hand. "I don't date employees."

"That's an excuse. You weren't interested."

"I am now," he told her simply.

Her tone was flat but her eyes flashed with heat and annoyance. "You liked the sex."

He nodded agreement. "And I like you."

"You didn't even know it was me until the blind-fold slipped," she countered.

Quinn would have to be an idiot not to see that she

was hurting but he didn't understand why. However, he knew Maggie well enough to know that she didn't get upset easily. So he schooled himself to patience. "I didn't know your name, true. But I knew you had a giving nature that's full of fun and a zest for life."

"That's just lust."

Was she going to make some demand on him in order to keep up their relationship? Quinn steeled himself, waiting for her to ask him for something. "What we have is more than lust. Tell me, Maggie, why did you take Laine's place?"

"I had this idiotic idea that I was infatuated with you, and that after we made love, I'd be ready to move on."

Well, that sounded honest. He was flattered that Maggie had initiated a personal relationship between them, pleased that it was working out so well. And he wanted more. "But after we made love at the hotel, you phoned me. Why?"

Maggie's voice was sad, her expression wistful. "Because you pranced—"

"Men don't prance."

"—into the office the next morning telling me how wonderful our night had been, so I figured, why not hook up again? I never meant for you to learn who I was."

Quinn had a difficult time believing that. "Why not?"

"Well, at first," she bit her lip, "I worried that you might fire me."

Huh? "Fire you?"

"For pulling off that kind of deception. But then I figured that we had such a good time that..."

Here it comes. He'd had such a good time that he'd give her anything she asked him for?

"I figured out later that you probably wouldn't fire me."

"Of course not. That wouldn't be very kind of me after all the pleasure you've given me," he teased.

Maggie sighed and drew her hand from his. She stood and paced. "You said you brought me here because you wanted to be with me."

"Yes." The best times he'd had this year had been with Maggie. Change that. The best times in his life had been with Maggie. He enjoyed working with her, depended on her to keep his business life working smoothly. But even more important, she made him eager to get out of bed in the morning to see just what she'd planned next. Practical Maggie was the most exciting woman he'd ever known.

She strode back and forth furiously, then halted and boldly placed her hands on her hips to face him. "So where exactly are we going from here?"

He wasn't quite sure what she was asking him, but tried to answer anyway. "I thought we'd work together. You'd help me to convince Laine to star in my next movie, and at night we'd be together."

"I don't think so."

Her defiant tone surprised him, shocked him, taunted him, almost as much as her words. Apparently she intended to give him the brush-off. "So you're done with me?"

"Yes."

She sounded very sure, but unhappy. Miserable even, so he didn't have a clue why she was ending things between them. Not that he intended to let her go. She meant too much to him, this Maggie who didn't want any favors, who gave of herself without asking for anything in return. He loved her, but sensed she wasn't ready to hear him say the words. Hell, he could barely believe them himself. Yet, he couldn't deny his feelings any more than he could cease living. He loved her. And he was quite pleased with himself for acknowledging the emotion when he'd never felt it before, never *wanted* to feel it before.

No way was she dumping him. That was an experience for other men, not Quinn. An experience that wouldn't sit well on his shoulders. Quinn wouldn't give her up without a battle. And Maggie had no idea how stubborn he planned to be. Going after what he wanted was his forte. And he wanted Maggie in his life day and night—forever.

He accepted the strength of his feelings for her with the same equanimity he accepted his most brilliant movie concepts. When he was right, he could feel it. And Maggie was right. He had no doubts whatsoever.

Positive that he could convince her to change her mind if he kept her talking, he gave her an opening to explain. "I don't understand."

She practically threw her words at him. "I planned on us having a fling. We had one. Now it's over."

"Because I learned it was you?"

"I don't owe you any explanations." Tears brimmed in her eyes and she turned away from him.

Quinn rose to his feet, took her into his arms, enjoying her soft, trembling skin. She didn't struggle, but she didn't melt against him, either. "Maggie, why are you ending what we've found together?"

"Because you aren't what I want. Don't you understand? We are wrong for each other. And I don't want to spend more time with a man that can't be part of my future."

Whoa.

She'd just thrown way more at him than he could digest all at once. He ignored that her earlier admission about being infatuated with him contradicted her more recent statement that he wasn't what she wanted. He honed in on her belief that he was wrong for her. How dare she tell him that. What was wrong with him anyway? Besides, he trusted his instincts. The woman he was holding was very right for him.

Yet, he kept his tone gentle. "Who says we are wrong for each other?"

"I do."

"And that's based on…?"

"I'm practical and a planner."

"So am I or I wouldn't be successful."

"You fly by the seat of your pants."

"Sometimes. I don't see the problem."

"I'm not a star. You are. And I don't want to spend my life trying to be what I'm not."

"Did you ever think that I like you the way you are?"

"Yeah, right. In the four years we've known each other, you never once thought about asking me out.

Now you expect me to believe that you like me the way I am? Don't insult my intelligence, please.''

Quinn restrained a smile. Even when Maggie told him off she was polite. "Maggie have you ever taken a trip to Europe? To Paris?''

"I've never been to Europe.''

"That doesn't matter. You dream of climbing the Eiffel Tower, walking down the Champs Elysee, seeing Notre Dame and floating on a river cruise down the Seine. But your plane has engine trouble and you land in Iceland. You can sit in the airport and fume about your lost time in Paris, or you can explore Iceland. Enjoy a different culture. Wander through the fishing communities. Visit a glacier. And finally the plane is repaired and you go to Paris—but the best part of your trip was Iceland where you were stuck on a bus next to a seventy-five-year-old lady who reminded you of your grandmother.''

"Are you comparing me to Iceland?''

He shook his head.

She looked at him suspiciously. "I don't remind you of your grandmother, do I?''

He failed to restrain a chuckle. "Hardly. What I'm saying is I might not have planned on us getting together—''

"You never even thought about it—''

"But now that we have—''

"Now that I tricked you into making love to me.''

"I'm glad that you did.''

"So we can keep doing what we've been doing?''

"Exactly.'' He was pleased that he'd calmed her, and convinced her that they could remain together.

And suddenly he understood why he got up in the mornings looking forward to every day. Maggie. The reason making love had become so special, so exciting. Maggie. The words that slipped from him so easily felt right and true. "I love you, Maggie."

"No, you don't." Every muscle in her body tensed for battle as she hardened her tone. "You're in lust. There's a difference."

"Yes, there is. And I know the difference."

"Oh, really." Her eyes flared with anger and a hint of vulnerability.

"You're scared, so you're running away from me. I love you," he repeated. "We're good together."

"No, we aren't. We work well together and we have great sex. And I refuse to believe that you even know what love is. Hell, you don't even have a pet. You could change your mind about us tomorrow— and that's not love, that's infatuation and lust."

She'd just said no to him again. But she shouldn't have. His reasoning was sound and logical. And he'd told her he loved her. Maybe she hadn't heard him. So he tried one more time. "Why can't you believe that I love you?"

Maggie yanked back from his embrace and he let her go. He wanted to see her eyes, but she avoided his gaze. "Quinn, I think you'd better go."

"I'm not going anywhere." He spoke calmly despite the anger running through his veins. Quinn's expert negotiating skills seemed ineffective with Maggie, but if she wouldn't respond to logic, or his arms around her, as her boss, he could keep her in his company until he decided on a new strategy.

"Don't try to push me around, Quinn," she warned as if reading his mind.

"Look, we still need dinner and I'd like to talk with you about how best to approach Laine. But first I want you to answer my question."

"Which question?"

"Why can't you believe that I love you?"

She tossed her hair back from her face as her head jerked up. Her blue eyes blazed with passion and anger and unreleased tears. "Fine. You love me. Prove it."

Aha. She'd just given him an opening. Although how he could prove he loved her eluded him at the moment. When he remained silent, he could read the unhappiness in her eyes and wondered what he could say to make it disappear. Showering her with kisses that began at her toes and ended on those deliciously scowling lips crossed his mind. But she'd call that lust, not love.

"How would you like to cast my next movie?"

For a nanosecond, her eyes fired with excitement but then narrowed in disdain. "That offer only proves you respect my business judgment, not that you love me."

"Are you turning down the job?"

"What do you think?"

"I think you should take some time to make up your mind." Quinn may have just lost ground with her, but her refusal to jump at his offer made his pulse leap. His head had doubted that Maggie was the real thing, a woman who wanted him for more than what he could give her professionally, but his heart knew better. He shouldn't have doubted her. But he hadn't anticipated that she'd be frightened of her own feelings. Not for one moment did he doubt that she had those feelings or she wouldn't have pursued him in the first place. Maggie couldn't just sweep into his life like a tidal wave and then ebb away with the tide. Quinn refused to lose her. Despite his frustration and this momentary setback, he had no doubt that he would succeed in changing her mind about him. Just as soon as he figured out how the heck a man proved his love.

He might not be able to define his emotions. The feeling was new to him, but that didn't mean his emotion wasn't real. Wasn't rare.

He would find a way to prove this feeling blooming in him, like the rarest flower, was love.

And he would enjoy the challenge.

10

HE LOVED HER?

Oh, God! What had she done?

Those words from him were the last ones she'd wanted to hear. Quinn had to be confused by the great sex.

Somehow, Maggie had gotten through dinner. Quinn had taken her to an exclusive restaurant that overlooked the harbor. He'd acted the perfect gentlemen, not pressing her, keeping the conversation on business. But she'd been too upset to taste the food she'd placed in her mouth. It didn't help that Quinn looked devastatingly attractive in his navy suit and dark maroon tie.

Never before had any of her plans gone so awry. And emotionally weary of trying to pretend she was fine, she'd ended their evening early to return to her hotel room.

She had some hard thinking to do—not the least of which was whether or not to accept Quinn's offer to cast his movie. This opportunity might never come her way again. Quinn the expert negotiator had just offered her a dream on a twenty-four-carat gold platter. But she couldn't deal with her career until she settled her rioting emotions.

Quinn had told her he loved her. But he didn't love her, of course. He couldn't possibly love her. Not because she wasn't lovable but because a man didn't just treat a woman like a secretary for four years and then fall in love with her in less than a week. The notion was absurd. A preposterous change of heart even for a man as given to extremes as Quinn. Even if he had seemed perfectly sincere when he'd declared that he loved her, her practical side told her differently.

So instead of making her giddy and happy, his words had speared her with a pain that wouldn't go away. Quinn had been right when he'd accused her of being afraid. She was afraid to believe him. What rational woman wouldn't be? She didn't want to love a man that didn't do long-term. A man that had no experience in holding a relationship together. For one thing, she knew enough about his parents to realize he'd had no good examples in his life. Quinn wouldn't know love if it crept up his leg and bit him. So even if he believed everything he'd said, she knew better. And for another thing, Quinn had made up his mind so fast it made her thoughts spin. No one could be that sure, that fast. Not even Quinn.

She hadn't worn the blindfold when he'd asked, because as much as she'd have preferred to go on with their sexual fling, she'd needed to end it before her heart became involved. Maggie believed she could *choose* the man she would love and she would not choose Quinn. He was too handsome, too charming. Too powerful and wealthy. She didn't want her man to escort movie stars to premieres as casually as other men opened a door for a lady. She didn't want to have to compete with every starlet that came down the pike. She wanted a man from a stable background similar to her own. The idea of falling for Quinn and watching other women pursue him was not for her.

Better to guard her feelings and remember their fantastic sex as a fond memory. She would have preferred if Quinn had never learned her identity. Once he had, she couldn't just keep going on as they'd been. Quinn might be a fairy tale come true, but he wasn't "ever after" material.

However, she couldn't change—wouldn't change—what had happened between them. Now, she just had to decide if she wanted to keep her job as his personal assistant. She didn't think she could. She couldn't pretend that they hadn't made love. Nor could she ever forget their time together. Perhaps it was time for her to move on. Perhaps she should take Quinn up on his offer to cast his movie and then parlay that credential into a successful career change. Maybe find a partner to back the start up costs. Lord knows, she could. She had the contacts.

However, accepting Quinn's offer would mean maintaining a connection with the man himself. And she wasn't sure she could handle that. He'd accused her of being afraid of her own feelings, but he'd been wrong. She was simply being practical.

Yeah, but if she was just being practical, she wouldn't hesitate to accept his offer. She wouldn't pass up this opportunity.

She paced back and forth in front of the bed. Okay, so she was a little scared. Maybe more than a little.

But she could handle herself once she decided what she wanted to do.

She didn't see hanging on to Quinn as any kind of option. On the other hand, she probably shouldn't have challenged him. She knew how stubborn he could be. He might pursue her to prove to himself that no woman could turn him down.

Had she done so on purpose? Maggie dropped her head into her hands. Did she want him to pursue her? If she was absolutely honest with herself, did she really want him to give up on her?

With all her feelings tumbling as if they were turning somersaults, Maggie slipped under the covers. No way was she going to sleep. Especially when she imagined Quinn in his room, pacing, the television on, while he spoke into his cell phone to Europe or Asia, making deals. *He* wouldn't be rethinking every word they'd spoken to one another. *He* wouldn't be second-guessing his plans.

She wanted to go to him, ask him to hold her, because she really didn't like herself much at the moment. She'd created this mess and had no idea how to clean it up. When had her life turned so complicated? And what was she going to do?

Maggie tossed and turned, dreading tomorrow when she'd give Quinn her answer about casting the movie. If she took on the project, she wouldn't be able to keep working as his assistant. Her own office and the distance from him would be good. She couldn't imagine sitting just outside his office door, available for his every whim, having to watch him move on with his life without her.

For a moment, she almost let herself believe that maybe Quinn had been sincere. That maybe he knew what love was and that he had real feelings for her. That they could spend their lives together.

Don't be stupid.

She would be setting herself up for heartbreak. The kind that messed a woman up for a long time. Although Maggie didn't feel her biological clock ticking, didn't even know if she wanted children, she wouldn't waste time on a man who had no experience with love.

She was afraid Quinn might keep her around because she was handy. Because they could share a good working relationship and a good sex life. But that wasn't love. And it wasn't permanent. She didn't want to waste time on Quinn when the possibility of a future together seemed so impossible.

Perhaps she should turn down his offer to cast his movie and give up her job as his personal assistant. With Quinn's recommendation, she could find other work. Start over. Meet new people.

But Maggie had other ties, besides Quinn, to Simitar Studios. She and Kimberly were good friends and often ate lunch together. They wouldn't see each other as often if Maggie moved on. Nor could she help Kimberly get her script read, maybe produced. Although Maggie didn't have any say in whether a screenplay was turned into a movie, she did schedule Quinn's hours, remind him of his most exciting projects, help him find the right directors and camerapeople and editors. If she left, she would miss the power she had at Simitar Studios as much as the friends she'd made there. Starting over from scratch didn't appeal to Maggie as much now as when she'd headed for L.A. after college, leaving behind family and friends.

So what was she going to do?

MAGGIE ROUSED TO POUNDING on her door. Usually she awakened immediately, all brain cells running smoothly. Since she hadn't fallen asleep until the wee hours of the morning, when she forced open her eyes, it took a moment to get her bearings. She was in a hotel room. Alone. Last night Quinn and she had argued.

Her whole messy problem came slamming back into her head full force. The pounding on the door only aggravated her too-heavy head.

"Go away."

The door opened and Quinn came inside pushing a cart laden with food. How had he gotten a key card? *Never mind.* What was he doing here?

"Go away," she muttered again, pulling the pillow over her head.

The cart's wheels squeaked as Quinn rolled it beside her bed. "Time for breakfast, Maggie mine."

"Don't call me that."

"Okay, Maggie darling."

"I'm not your darling. I'm not your anything."

"That remains to be seen. I prefer to think positively. So no negative vibes, woman." When she didn't move or verbally respond, he coaxed, "Don't you want to see what I brought you?"

If he was trying to bribe her, his tactic was working. The delicious scent of coffee alone almost drove her out from under the pillow. But he hadn't just brought coffee. She smelled bacon and her mouth betrayed her by watering.

Her stomach rumbled, reminding her she hadn't eaten much last night. She sat up, pulling the sheet to her chin.

She glared at Quinn, but it was difficult to remain angry at him when she saw the feast he'd ordered. Waffles with fresh strawberries, blueberries and whipped cream. Orange juice with lots of pulp. Toasted muffins and hot croissants with little silver pots of jelly and butter. Eggs, fried, scrambled and poached. Granola with raisins. Milk. Pancakes with more berries. Sausage. Bacon And tea.

"You ordered enough food to feed ten people."

He shot her a charming grin. "I don't know what you like, so I ordered everything."

How like Quinn. She should have expected he'd do something excessive and outrageous. Naturally he didn't think twice about the cost. Or that she might throw him out. But it *would* be a shame to let all that wondrous food go to waste. Besides, she could see by the expression in Quinn's eyes, a glint of mischievousness, that he was up to something. And she needed to know what in order to counter him.

He flipped open a napkin and handed it to her. When she was slow to accept, he gently floated it over her lap, and she caught a whiff of his soap. He'd already showered, shaved and dressed for the day in buff-colored slacks and an emerald shirt that brought out the green in his eyes.

In comparison, she felt rumpled. Her hair was a mess and she'd yet to brush her teeth. But she wasn't getting out of bed in the nightgown she was wearing. Things had been different between them when Quinn had purchased the lacy violet garment for her. Last night, when her attire was the last thing on her mind, she'd worn it due to lack of any other choices.

"Coffee?" Quinn asked.

"Please."

He made hers black and handed her the cup. While she sipped, he placed three sugars and lots of cream in his. He picked up a plate and gestured to the food. "So what would you like?"

"An answer to why you are here."

"Food first. You didn't eat enough last night to fill a flea."

"First you compare me to Iceland. Now a flea. Really, Quinn, for a man who makes a living with words, you should choose them more carefully."

"I'll keep that in mind." His eyes twinkled and she realized too late he was teasing her to get a reaction. Damn him for being three steps ahead of her and looking so cool, collected and ready to cater to her every whim.

"The waffles look good," he urged her. "And there's honey and maple syrup."

She gave in. There was no point in sending him away. They were going to have to work together unless she ran away, which she really didn't want to do. "Okay. And some bacon, please."

Quinn filled her plate, then topped up her coffee before filling his own. While she balanced the plate on her lap, he pulled over his chair and dug into his food.

Maggie washed down a bite of bacon with orange juice. "All right. Tell me why you're here."

"You told me to prove that I loved you."

Maggie stifled a groan. "If you think that ordering an outrageous breakfast is proof of your feelings, then you have a lot to learn about love."

"To prove my feelings, we have to be together."

"What?" She jerked up her head so fast, she almost spilled the coffee on the way to her lips.

Quinn's eyes lit with amusement. "Well, after sifting through my memory of the best romance movies of all time, it occurred to me that love can't be proven from a distance. We have to spend more time together."

Maggie set down her coffee cup on the nightstand. She'd known she'd made a mistake the moment she'd challenged Quinn. The man thrived on contests of will, but she'd never dreamed he would focus such interest on *her.*

He'd spent last night coming up with a way to spend more time with her while she'd been trying to figure out the opposite. The irony wasn't lost on her, but she couldn't summon even the beginnings of a smile. Quinn was one of those men who enjoyed writing a story differently, using camera angles that were original, marketing ideas that were innovative. And then he moved on to his next project—just as he would eventually become bored with her and move on to the next woman. That was his nature—to concentrate fully, get what he wanted. Then, predictably, something new would capture his attention. So she couldn't let him get that close. Her self-preservation instincts were too good to set herself up for that kind of fall.

"You're very quiet," he prodded.

"And you're backing me into a corner."

"I'm feeding you breakfast, and you aren't eating enough." He offered her the basket of muffins.

She took one and broke it into pieces. She wasn't going to argue with Quinn until she found out exactly what he was thinking. Of course, with Quinn, he never laid all his cards on the table. He always had a plan B, C, D and E. And he usually had an ulterior motive. However, by stating his plan to spend time with her, he was declaring his intention to pursue her and that was enough to deal with at the moment.

Before Maggie had pretended to be Laine Lamonde, she might have welcomed his attention. But now? Quinn wasn't accustomed to women saying no to him. She fully believed Quinn was enjoying the challenge of pursuit. He was in lust.

"How much time were you thinking we should spend together?" she asked.

He speared a piece of pineapple and popped it into his mouth. "I don't think we can put a time limit on love, do you?"

"You're being evasive."

"I don't suppose you're ready to move into my house—"

Move in with him? She almost choked on the muffin. Move in with him? She didn't even know if she wanted to have dinner with him and he was thinking about living together.

Take a breath. Think. Even Quinn had qualified his suggestion by acknowledging she wasn't ready to live together.

"So, I was thinking about six nights a week."

"Six nights?"

"Plus all day on the weekends, of course."

"Are you out of your mind?"

"I'm in love."

"You're certifiable. Even married couples don't spend that much time together."

"Five nights, all day Saturday and Sunday morning," he countered.

"Two nights and Saturday afternoon would be more reasonable."

Oh, God. What had she done? How had he gotten her bargaining with him when she hadn't intended to go along with his scheme in the first place? Too late, her hand slapped against her mouth.

He nodded his head, keeping his face stoic, but his eyes glimmered with satisfaction. "I want more. But I can live with two nights and Saturday afternoons," he agreed. "But I expect the nights to be all-night."

"What!" Another man would have proved his love wasn't lust by curtailing or ceasing their lovemaking. But not Quinn. Oh, no. He wanted to continue to wear down her barriers by making love to her, coming at her with everything he had, everything he was. Not good, not for her.

Quinn must have read the worry on her face.

His tone was gentle, almost sympathetic. "Don't

worry, Maggie darling. I'm not going to force you to do anything you don't want to do.''

That's what she was afraid of.

Oh, God.

Quinn finally grinned, arrowing heat straight to the sudden throbbing between her thighs. ''If you don't want to wear that blindfold, I'll understand.''

Feeling entangled in a trap that she wasn't sure she wanted to escape, Maggie didn't know whether to laugh or to cry. And Quinn being Quinn, he gave her no time to think. He removed her plate, took out a book full of men's faces and dumped it on her lap. ''If we're going to find some leading man for Laine to choose from before our noon meeting with her, we'd best get started.''

Maggie tossed the book back at him. ''First, I'm going to brush my teeth and shower.''

''Can I watch?''

''And you are going to wait in the lobby,'' she demanded, irritably.

He leaned over and brushed his lips against hers. ''You don't have to fight me all the time, Maggie darling.''

''Don't call me that.''

''I'll leave you to your shower. Alone.''

She didn't relax until he'd shut the door and she'd slid the chain into place. Then she marched to the bathroom, determined not to come out until she figured out how to deal with Quinn.

By lunchtime, Maggie had come to no good conclusion about her situation, but as she and Quinn waited for Laine Lamonde to show up at their luncheon meeting, Maggie was glad the star would be joining them. She didn't want to be alone with Quinn until she'd put her thoughts in order.

And she'd spent the morning making lists of roles and thinking about who could play each part to get the most out of the character. Who would look good matched with whom. Who might be free to work during the shooting. And how to get the most out of the budget Quinn had allotted. Although she had yet to officially accept Quinn's offer, she much preferred to think about how to cast his movie than her personal quandary.

After ten tense minutes, Maggie's nerves were fraying raw from sitting across from a relaxed Quinn. Finally the star and her agent, Tyrol, showed. Every eye in the room focused on Laine. In an industry of gorgeous woman, she could be number one, her charisma sparkling around her like a golden halo. Even dressed down in gold designer jeans and a cream T-shirt threaded with gold and crystal beads, Laine wore stiletto heels. Her famous blond locks had that just-out-of-bed natural look that took hours to achieve. And she walked with the grace of a runway model, every move precise and feminine, drawing attention to her swaying hips.

Eyes on the star, Quinn rose to his feet, his face polite but far from awestruck. But then Maggie didn't expect anything less. To Quinn, beautiful women were a common commodity, what he really admired was acting ability.

Laine took her time crossing the room, giving

Quinn a chance to assess her perfect body and thousand-watt smile. When she finally arrived at their table, she hugged Quinn with what appeared to be genuine warmth, but her cold blue eyes glared at Maggie, making her feel as if she didn't exist.

Tough. Quinn wanted her to be here. And if she accepted the casting director's job, Maggie would need to feel out Laine's preferences in leading men.

"So glad we can finally meet."

Laine spoke with no French accent at all. Maggie snorted quietly to herself, recalling all the trouble she'd gone to to mimic an accent that didn't exist.

Quinn swiftly made introductions all-round, introducing Maggie as his casting director as if she'd already accepted the work. He had a way of plunging ahead that kept her off balance. But Maggie kept her thoughts to herself. Personal squabbles had no place at this table which was strictly a business meeting. Besides, she might very well accept the opportunity Quinn had placed at her feet.

Laine's agent was short, overweight and bald. Unfortunately Tyrol didn't have the puppy dog eyes of a Danny DeVito. His ears were too big and his bulbous nose was reddened, maybe from too much alcohol. And his eyes watched everyone at the table like a wise owl.

"First I must thank you for rescuing my Molly. She was so happy to see me."

"Maggie found her."

"When you gave the customs people the studio's address, the dog was accidentally mixed into some animals we needed for a movie," Maggie explained.

"My poor baby."

Maggie noted that Laine didn't thank her and let it go. "I was glad to help and she was well treated."

A waitress interrupted the conversation, pouring water into their glasses. After she left, Quinn changed the topic of conversation.

"What do you think of the part of Kiki?" Quinn asked Laine, referring to the lead character in the script.

In the film, Kiki went from a child seductress to successful businesswoman. She married, divorced and along the way, she suffered from a mental breakdown. She ended up institutionalized, but fought her way back to sanity. The part required an actress who could play a woman from her teens to her sixties with not only convincing accuracy but deep emotional depth.

Laine bit off a piece of her sesame breadstick. "I'm not sure."

"About what?" Quinn prodded.

"Whether I want to be seen as quite that old, ugly and wacko. Perhaps, you could tone down that part just a bit?"

Quinn didn't blink one eyelash that the woman had just suggested he tear out the heart of the script. "What are you suggesting?"

Laine waved her manicured nails in the air, then placed her hand intimately on Quinn's shoulder. "You are the writer. Surely you can figure out a way for me to—?"

"Stay forever young, sane and beautiful?" Quinn asked, his tone mild, but Maggie heard the sarcasm beneath.

Laine didn't. "Exactly!"

"For you, I would rewrite the screenplay, but it would hurt your chances of winning an Academy Award." Leave it to Quinn to appeal to the woman's self-interests. He was so good at that.

"Really?" Laine turned to her agent.

Apparently Tyrol didn't speak unless invited to do so by his famous client. He sipped his wine then set his glass down carefully. "Oscar-winning actresses and nominees take emotional, gut-wrenching parts. Remember Halle Berry in *Monster's Ball?* Or Susan Sarandon in *Dead Man Walking?*"

"But why can't I be pretty while I show emotional depth?"

Maggie refrained from rolling her eyes at the ceiling. Laine might be gorgeous and she might be a great actress, but clearly she didn't understand what made audiences go to the movies. Sure, the public liked pretty actresses—but they expected them to act in a compelling story.

"I'll think about it," Quinn told her but Maggie and her agent both knew he wouldn't change the script. "Now, Laine, tell me who you want for your leading men. You'll have three. A teenage lover when you're younger, then a husband and a distinguished man at the end of the movie."

"How about Ben Affleck, you and your father?" Laine ticked off the men on her fingers.

"I don't act."

"You're acting right now. You're patronizing me. Do you think I'm stupid?" Laine's eyes flared as she raised her voice in ire, drawing the other customers' gazes to her. "Don't you think I know you aren't going to change the script? I don't want to be ugly and old."

"Magnificent." Quinn complimented her. "Can you summon up that self-righteous anger at will?"

Laine giggled. "Of course." Her hand clasped Quinn's forearm and she let a finger trace down to his wrist. "Are you sure you don't want to act opposite me?"

"I couldn't do you justice."

Maggie fought to keep a grin from showing.

"And Dad is under contract to another film—"

"Buy out his contract."

Maggie spoke up. "That might be possible, but then we'd have to use up the funds we've already allocated for the historical sets and costumes so necessary to create a great period film." Maggie eyed Laine carefully. "What do you think about Todd Landon?"

"Who?" Laine addressed the question to Quinn.

Maggie handed Laine an eight-by-ten color head shot of the handsome male star whose popularity couldn't be questioned. He'd been out of circulation the last two years nursing a wife who'd succumbed to breast cancer, but was now looking for the right project.

Laine tossed the photo back. "He's fair skinned."

"And?"

Her agent sighed. "Laine doesn't work with men whose skin is fairer than hers. And no blondes."

"She doesn't want any of her leading men to be blond?" Maggie asked to clarify.

"No other blondes, men or women, in the picture," Tyrol spoke as if Maggie was supposed to know this. "Not secondary characters. Not even walk-ons."

Maggie looked at Quinn, unsure how to respond. He smoothly took over. "I'm sure we can work around that requirement."

But it sure wasn't going to be easy. Mentally Maggie scratched a few actresses off her list.

"If you want me, you'll need to work around all my requirements," Laine told him, sliding her hand onto Quinn's thigh. Her maneuver wasn't meant to be cute or coy or secret.

Quinn took her hand from his leg and placed it back on the table. And he was just as blunt. "As desirable as I find you, I never mix business and pleasure."

Maggie cringed at the first part, but she knew he had to let Laine down easy. The woman was so accustomed to getting her man that, for a moment, her lower jaw dropped.

Maggie restrained an outright laugh. She also appreciated how uncomfortable Quinn must be feeling. He was sitting next to Maggie, his recent lover, while he had to reject Laine's invitation, without hurting anyone's feelings.

However, Quinn looked as in control and comfortable as usual. His eyes twinkled as if he was pleased to be talking to the star, yet his manner conveyed a firmness that told Laine exactly where she stood with him.

Laine pouted. "You won't act with me in your

film, and you won't party with me. That's not what I would call a warm welcome.''

Quinn leaned toward her and lowered his voice as if conveying a secret. "Do you know a certain red-head's agent called me just last week and asked if Kiki's part had been cast yet?" Quinn leaned back. "I told the agent the part had been offered to another actress."

"Of course, I'm perfect for the role," Laine added.

"You will be a sensation," Quinn told her.

"Darling, I'm always a sensation."

Laine's gaze went to Tyrol, signaling him that she wanted him to speak. "Quite frankly, we have another interesting offer."

"From Dan O'Donnel?" Quinn spoke as casually as if that was last week's news. "His movie is not as big as mine. The part of playing a role like Kiki's will come along only once in a lifetime. And I've lined up a terrific director for you—one of the best—"

"Wait, just a damn minute." Laine raised her voice again. "I was under the impression that *you* were going to direct."

"John Davis loves your work," Quinn began and Maggie realized how truly terrific he was as a negotiator—because Quinn had planned all along to co-direct this film with John Davis. No doubt he would eventually agree to Laine's demand to help direct her film—but it would appear as if he'd made a major concession.

And as the negotiations went on, Maggie wondered how she could ever hold out against a determined Quinn. Or even if she wanted to.

11

MAGGIE RETURNED TO THE HOTEL room and did something she rarely had the luxury to do; she took an afternoon nap. She awakened several hours later to knocking at her door. Completely rejuvenated, though no closer to solving her dilemma over what to do about Quinn, she bounced out of bed, checked through the peephole and spied the bellhop holding a huge basket of flowers, chocolates and champagne.

Maggie opened the door to the scent of lilies. The basket was ostentatious, and her heart couldn't help softening at Quinn's romantic gesture. He'd ordered the flowers himself. She tipped the bellhop and reached for the note.

Maggie read aloud. "It's Saturday night. Wear the blindfold for me, Maggie. I'll pick you up at seven. Love, Quinn."

She liked Quinn's persistence because it meant he believed his feelings for her were serious. But she also disliked his persistence because he was hitting her with another surprise before she'd dealt with the last. His tactic to overwhelm her was keeping her off balance, which made resisting him more difficult.

She thought about drinking the entire bottle of champagne so she could blame the alcohol for doing as he asked and acting irresponsibly. Then she could wear the blindfold and have a delicious night of sex with Quinn without making up her mind. But that would be taking the easy way out.

Nothing wrong with the easy way, Maggie girl.

It wasn't as if making love to him again was committing to more than a continuation of the fling she'd wanted. But Maggie knew that the more intimate time that she spent with Quinn, the harder it would be to guard her feelings. And her self-protective instincts were strong. They'd been strong enough to keep her from going after Quinn for the last four years. But not strong enough to keep her out of the mess she'd created. Now that she'd broken down the physical barrier between them, keeping her heart out of the mix wasn't such an easy task.

Maggie leaned into the lilies and breathed deeply. She loved fresh-cut flowers and chocolate and champagne. Who didn't? But that didn't mean she would automatically succumb to Quinn's request.

But she wanted to. And fighting her own desires along with his was really more than a woman should have to do. Just because he'd tricked her into bargaining with him earlier didn't mean she had to go along with his plans. Neither did taking the casting opportunity he'd offered. Or the flowers, chocolates and champagne. All of those gestures were wonderful, but none of them meant that he really loved her, did they?

She'd asked him to prove his love and he'd certainly taken the challenge seriously. But she had no idea how one proved love—or trust, which was really the issue. She couldn't read his mind—only her own. And even without the champagne, her thoughts seemed fuzzy around the edges. She admired Quinn. She adored making love with him. She liked working with him. But that wasn't enough. To let herself love him, she needed to know that he loved her. But how could he prove that? Had she set him an impossible task, so she'd be free to walk away? Was she really as afraid as he'd said?

Maggie didn't know.

She lifted the blindfold off the nightstand and ran it through her fingers. Was he right that she had to give him a chance? She didn't know that, either. In fact ever since she'd begun her quest to make love with Quinn, her IQ seemed to have plunged.

Yet, as seven o'clock approached, she found herself showering and dressing, still not committed to the night with him. At five to seven, she wondered if she was making the biggest mistake of her life as she tied the blindfold over her eyes.

Yet, once she did, she knew that she couldn't fight what she wanted and him, too. The five minutes ticked by too fast, and at the knocking on her door, her mouth went dry.

She licked her lips. "Come in."

She heard him step inside and close the door. Sensed him watching her. Smelled his clean scent that made her think of rolling around the crisp hotel sheets with him. "Thanks for the flowers."

"You're welcome. You have no idea how I enjoyed the thought of you blindfolded, waiting here for me."

His rich voice alone heated her, but then his words actually set off a pulse between her thighs. Her breasts ached for his touch and her nipples hardened as if her body recognized the love her mind had yet to accept.

And she finally believed she'd made the right decision. There was no place she'd rather be right now than here with Quinn, anticipating what he'd planned for their evening. If things didn't work out between them, at least she hadn't fled out of cowardice. She was here, ready for him to sweep her into another rich sexual fantasy.

"Ready to go?" he asked as if she wasn't wearing a blindfold, as if he had no idea how much she wanted him to take her into his arms and kiss her.

She wished she could see his face, wondered at his expression. He sounded as if he'd moved fairly close to her but she couldn't be certain.

Talking when she wasn't sure exactly where he was seemed strange to her. Exciting somehow. "We're going out?"

"Oh, yes."

"But I'm wearing a blindfold."

His tone was light and playful but edged with desire. "If anyone asks, I'll tell them it's your birthday, and I'm planning a surprise present."

She grinned as she realized he was as impatient to have her as she was to have him. Perhaps she could keep him in this room, after all. "Well, if you're going to be responsible for me, there's something you should know."

"What's that?"

"We forgot to buy lingerie." She heard him take a ragged breath. "So I'm not wearing anything under my skirt."

At her words, her pulse accelerated. She couldn't help wondering if the thought of her so bare, so accessibly close by, caused him to harden. She wouldn't mind changing his plans and coaxing him into making love right here, right now.

As if reading her mind, he spoke softly. "You know Maggie, I think you should show me."

Huh? In her desire to get him to make love to her, she hadn't been following the conversation. "Show you what?"

"Lift your skirt for me, babe."

And all of a sudden what she was doing hit her like an icy bucket of water, causing her spine to shiver. Quinn had seen every inch of her—but back then he hadn't known that she was Maggie. And that made the prospect of lifting her skirt so different that she hesitated. Panicked. Tried to change the subject. "I thought we were going out."

"We will. But I want to see what's under that skirt. A little appetizer."

"Wouldn't you rather use your imagination?"

"What happened to my bold lover?"

For a moment, her obvious reluctance seemed to surprise Quinn, but then he finally seemed to realize this was the first time Maggie was with him as Maggie. She didn't have her fake French character to hide behind. And trusting him was different when he could reject *her,* not some character she was playing.

"It's not so easy when the blindfold is over *your* eyes, is it?" he asked.

She told herself that she was ridiculous to feel so vulnerable. Not five minutes ago she'd wanted to make love and would have tossed off her clothes without any need to convince herself that she shouldn't be naked with this man. But the entire scenario with him fully dressed and her partially so—suddenly had her wondering what she was doing.

Did she want to make love?

Yes.

Did she want Quinn to see her?

Yes.

Did she want Quinn to touch her?

Absolutely.

Yet just thinking about lifting her skirt while he looked at her when she couldn't see him had her nerves snapping. She recalled when he'd waited for her in his office—completely nude. And how he'd pursued her relentlessly *after* finding out her true identity. The memory gave her a measure of courage mixed with a bolt of desire.

Perhaps he did have real feelings for her.

Standing on trembling legs, she clenched and unclenched her fingers. She inhaled and exhaled, trying to calm her galloping breath. Then slowly she lifted her skirt. Very slowly. Inch by revealing inch, she showed him her knees, her thighs, her almost totally shaved mons, so silkily bare.

And very lightly, he skimmed his fingers up the inside of her smooth thighs. She'd never felt more naughty in her life, and she was loving every second of wondering what he'd do next. Where he'd touch next.

His breath fanned her thigh and she realized he must be kneeling at her feet. "You know what I'm remembering, Maggie? How you teased me when I was the one blindfolded."

She sucked in a breath of air, waiting in anticipation for his first touch, his first kiss.

"You undressed for me, but I couldn't watch you then," he coaxed. "But I can see you now, Maggie. I like looking at you and knowing I can slip my tongue between your folds, run my hands over your bottom or just taunt you with my breath fanning over your skin. And you're enjoying every moment. You want me here with you, don't you?"

She did. In fact, her skin was already plumping for him in expectation.

"Of course I want you." Maggie's hesitation was gone. "And I want you to do more than look."

She parted her thighs slightly. She was already damp. Wanting him.

It was his turn to draw in hot air.

And she thought that if he didn't touch her soon she would just keel over and collapse.

Luckily for her, he couldn't resist fondling her. He slipped his fingers into her slick folds. Then stopped. Stopped way too soon. What had happened to his fingers slicking back her flesh and his mouth on her? Why wasn't he doing anything?

"What's wrong?" she asked.

"Perhaps, I'm jumping a few steps. I intended to

kiss you first, play with your breasts. I'm going too fast—''

''You aren't.'' At his sudden cessation of love-making, she felt like gnashing her teeth in frustration.

''Room service.'' At the knock on the door, she jumped and smoothed down her skirt, making sure she was totally covered up from prying eyes.

Quinn paid the bellhop and returned to Maggie. ''I asked room service to bring up this special lotion. Lift your skirt again.''

This time his tone was more commanding, sexy. She wanted the need back in his tone. After all, if they were going to play love games, she didn't want to do so in frustrating fits and starts. But he wasn't going to change his mind. She'd heard that in his firm determination to put the lotion on her.

She bit her bottom lip, but didn't hesitate to lift the skirt. She imagined him unscrewing the cap and dabbing the lotion onto his fingers. When he touched her, she still jumped.

''It's cold.''

He smoothed the lotion over her mons. ''How does that feel?''

''How is it supposed to feel?'' she answered impatiently.

''Just wait.'' She could hear the water splashing in the bathroom sink and figured he must be washing the lotion off of his hands. ''The bottle says to reapply as needed.''

''I'm tingly.''

''Reapply ever hour or so. I think I'm going to

enjoy this,'' he teased and she suspected he was enjoying the blush that heated her neck.

When she started to lower her skirt again, he grabbed her wrist. ''Let me blow the lotion dry, Maggie.''

''What did you put on me?''

''An aphrodisiac.''

''There's no such thing.''

''If you say so. However, you should begin to feel warm down there quite soon.'' He skimmed a finger up the inside of her thigh and slipped it onto her clit. ''I adore pink.''

''Are you trying to embarrass me.''

''I've already seen all of you. And I like what I see.''

''But—''

He moved his finger ever so slowly over her clit, making her wild with need. ''Trusting isn't so easy when the blindfold's on you, is it?'' he teased softly.

Trusting wasn't easy for her, period. Oh my the things the man could do with just one finger. ''I can't take—''

''You're strong, Maggie. A lot stronger than either of us knew. Have I ever told you how much I adore strong women?''

His finger was making it almost impossible not to gyrate her hips.

And he knew how he was driving her wild. Damn him, he knew. ''Hold still, Maggie. You don't want to get that lotion on your pretty skirt, do you?''

''Surely I must be dry by now?''

''Almost.''

His finger moved just the tiniest bit faster. Maggie bit her lip but failed to keep back a moan. She would have been a fool to pass up another night together. Another fantastic orgasm. She thought Quinn might stop, leave her hanging. But he just kept playing, so gently that the explosion sneaked up on her. It wasn't a huge orgasm, but it lasted and lasted and lasted. Quinn never broke contact and never stopped moving his finger until she staggered. She would have fallen if he hadn't caught her up in his arms.

"Just think, sweetheart—"

She didn't want to think.

"We can do that over and over. I believe the package said to reapply every hour."

Every hour? He intended to give her an orgasm every hour? "Surely you can't be serious?"

"Oh, but I am."

"But—"

"I didn't forget to buy you underwear, Maggie," he told her sounding quite pleased with himself.

"You planned to, to…"

"I'm going to enjoy seeing how many times I can make you come in one evening."

He pulled down her skirt for her. "It's time to go."

"Go?"

"I told you before that we're going out."

"I thought—"

"That I'd changed my mind?"

"Well, you did say you were going to reapply the lotion, so I assumed—"

"You assumed incorrectly."

"We're really not going to make love?" She couldn't hide the disappointment in her voice.

"First, we're taking a walk, then having dinner."

"And then we're going to make love?"

Deliberately, he didn't answer. She knew Quinn was having way too much fun to satisfy her curiosity yet. Anticipation would undoubtedly add to both of their eventual pleasure, but not knowing what he planned was setting her nerves on edge.

"Quinn, I'm not into taking my clothes off in public."

"Let's just see how the night unfolds."

Maggie couldn't imagine going that far, but then she should have been satisfied with the wonderful orgasm he'd given her yet she wanted more. The tension rebuilding between her legs, plus the sheer exhilaration of the moment, had carried her into a place she'd never been. Always before when she'd been with Quinn, she'd had her anonyminity to protect her. When Quinn hadn't known her identity, she'd felt as if there could be no lasting consequences of their love play. She could always change her mind and still have had the security of knowing that he'd never know what had really happened between them.

Now, she could no longer hide. He'd made that abundantly clear just moments ago.

And just knowing he intended to give her more orgasms kindled a heat that even now kept her moist with wanting.

She didn't know what exactly about Quinn could excite her into this state of heightened sexuality. Maggie wasn't inexperienced. She'd had other lovers, although her last serious relationship had been before she'd turned thirty—over two years ago. With her last boyfriend, she'd had no complaints in the sex department, but he couldn't make her pulse leap the way Quinn could.

Quinn led her out of her hotel room toward the elevator. She was surprised when they descended toward the lobby. She'd have thought he might be bringing her up to his private suite for dinner, but he walked her right through the hotel lobby and outside into the cool night air and the sidewalk.

"Now you need to take a large step up," he directed her.

Maggie did as he asked, a maneuver made easier with Quinn's guidance on her foot as he placed it squarely on a step.

Maggie smelled the clean animal scent of a horse and she was delighted that he'd apparently rented a buggy and driver to take them around the city. And yet since this was her first visit to Vancouver, she would have liked to have seen where they were going, but she wouldn't spoil Quinn's plans by asking to remove the blindfold.

"We're going for a ride in a carriage?"

"You'll find out soon enough." Quinn took the seat next to her and tucked a blanket over their laps. "And don't worry about the driver overhearing our conversation. I requested him because he's hard of hearing."

The driver must have signalled the horse because the buggy moved forward. Maggie enjoyed the sound of the horse's hooves on the road and snuggled against Quinn's shoulder. "I didn't know you could be so romantic."

He placed an arm over her shoulder and spoke into her ear with a husky tone. "I have an ulterior motive."

"And what would that be?"

"Seduction." Beneath the blanket, his fingers found the hem of her skirt and skimmed up her legs.

"I don't buy that excuse. You could have seduced me back at the hotel."

"But this is going to be much more…interesting," he promised while his fingers caressed lazy circles along her knee.

Cars whizzed past them, trucks honked and people spoke to one another along the sidewalks. But all she could think about was the breeze on her face, the sway of the carriage and Quinn's fingers dancing along her skin.

She tried to keep up a conversation. "Why is the carriage more interesting?"

"Because no matter how much I fire you up, we can't make love in it." His fingers dipped between her thighs.

"Oh."

"Exactly."

Already tendrils of excitement had her breasts aching for similar attention. She didn't know why she reacted so immediately to his every caress. Perhaps it was the lotion's effects on her. Perhaps the blindfold placed her in a world where she had to concentrate on her remaining senses. Quinn's clean male scent in addition to his mesmerizing voice and his wicked touch had her reeling in no time.

"Quinn, exactly how long is our carriage ride?"

"Long enough for us to get to talk." He inserted his fingertip inside her. "You know this whirlwind relationship hasn't included enough conversation."

He was teasing her thoroughly and the sway of the carriage seemed to heighten the effect of her already sensitive breasts. Without her bra, her breasts bobbed and her nipples rubbed her blouse increasing the ache between her legs.

"I can't even think while you're doing that."

"You can," he insisted. "And there's one question I'd really like an answer to." His fingers slowed to a disconcertingly minute pace.

"What?" Her voice came out breathlessly.

"Why don't you think we can be good together?"

She wriggled against his hand, hoping he'd give her a little more. And then she realized he was waiting for an answer that she didn't want to give.

"We are good together."

He stoked her clit, shooting a sizzling wave of heat to her core. The orgasm he'd given her in her room had only made her sensitive for more. He quickly brought her right to the edge of another. She released a gasp at the pure pleasure, forgetting everything but the wondrous sensation of his fingers.

"I mean, why don't you believe we can be good together on a more permanent basis?" he specified, his fingers once again frustratingly slow.

"Look at your history. What are the chances that you could ever stick it out with one woman?"

"So you're holding my parents' failed marriage against me?" His fingers began to move again, faster, quicker.

She finally caught on that he was subjecting her to this sweet torture to get to the truth. Already, her blood was rushing through her and her throat was tight. Breathing in air past her dry throat made talking difficult. Who could think clear thoughts when so aroused? Certainly not Maggie.

"Your background is only part of the problem."

"What else?"

"Your work."

His fingers played faster again but that didn't stop her from realizing her mistake. She'd admitted more than she'd intended.

Naturally a man known for negotiating with bankers and financiers immediately picked up on her error. "You disapprove of what I do for a living?"

She squirmed as his clever fingers kept teasing her. "I disapprove of the way women throw themselves at you. Beautiful, young women. I don't want to compete with that."

"You don't have to."

The carriage took a corner and she leaned a little to one side. Quinn took the opportunity to nudge his finger deeper inside her. His thumb on her clit was driving her wild and her breath came in soft pants.

"Quinn, no man is immune. If we stay together long enough, we'll have arguments and the idea of some hungry starlet waiting in the wings to console you is—"

"Ridiculous. Do you think I'm so shallow?"

She couldn't think, didn't want to say. Why couldn't he just let her enjoy what he was doing to her body? With her mind clouded with passion, she couldn't possibly choose her words carefully enough.

"Quinn, can't we talk later?"

"I don't think so." His voice was easy but his fingers were taking her to another peak.

"I just…wanted…a fling."

"You expect me to believe that?"

"It's the truth."

"When was the last time you had a fling?"

"I've never…not like this. I'm…going…to…"

Gently he pulled his hand from between her legs. "No, Maggie. I promised you one orgasm every hour and it's not yet time for you to come."

She groaned.

"I want to make you feel exactly how I felt after we had phone sex."

"Huh?"

"I want you crazy with need."

"But I am."

"I want you to wonder if and when you'll get satisfaction."

"But—"

"This time, you're going to have to wait."

She would have protested but the carriage had come to a stop. Were they back at the hotel? Would Quinn sweep her up to the room and make love to her? Her legs were so weak, she didn't know if she could walk.

"Thank you," Quinn said to someone on the sidewalk. The driver? She didn't know. She concentrated on drawing oxygen into her lungs, her thoughts swirling in hazy circles. She couldn't read Quinn's reaction to her admission. Was he annoyed that she didn't believe he could commit to any woman? Was he angry? He was so contained, she didn't have a clue and that added to her tension.

The delicious scent of hot potatoes wafted to her. Were they outside a restaurant?

In a moment, the carriage was moving forward again. And she could feel part of a tray resting on her thigh.

"Just a moment while I clean my hands. The hotel supplied steaming towels, would you care for one?"

"Please."

She expected him to hand her one. Instead he took the warm, damp towel and tenderly rubbed her wrists, her palms, between her fingers and over her knuckles. He followed up with another warm towel to dry, leaving her feeling clean, refreshed and pampered.

"Are you hungry?"

"Yes."

"Open your mouth," he ordered.

She did as he asked and he placed something warm and soft onto her tongue. When she bit into the fluff of pastry, potato and cheese filled her mouth. "Oh, that was good."

"How about a drink?"

He placed a straw between her lips and she sipped a light, tangy wine. They shared a variety of tiny puff pastries and the wine and then he kissed her, making her forget everything but his mouth. And every sensation in her body that had ebbed returned in full force.

Breathless once more after he finally broke their kiss, she snuggled against him and her hand wound its way into his lap. Gently, he removed her fingers.

"Uh-uh. You got to play in the bathtub, and with me when I was blindfolded. Tonight is my turn to play—and we're only beginning."

12

STILL BLINDFOLDED, Maggie could only judge the amount of time that had passed by the number of orgasms Quinn had given her. Three. Three orgasms, each more explosive than the last. And between times, they'd used hot towels to wash, paused long enough to stop and pick up delicious food, which Quinn fed her between sips of wine.

To outside eyes she was covered by a blanket, a skirt and a blouse, but Quinn had total access to every inch of her flesh. Quinn eased his hand under her blouse to fondle her breasts. "We're going somewhere unforgettable next."

When he tweaked her nipple, she let loose a tiny gasp. "I assure you that this carriage ride is a night I'll never forget."

"You're having a good time?"

"You have to ask?"

"I just want to hear you say so."

He had both hands under her blouse, plucking, stroking, caressing, making talking difficult. She was so sensitive that the tiniest touch had her quivering with anticipation and need.

"I'm having a good time, Quinn."

"Because the sex is good?" he asked, his lips nibbling her ear.

"Yes."

"And would you be here with me, blindfolded in a carriage, if you didn't trust me?"

"There are different kinds...of trust."

He tugged at her nipples and didn't stop, twirling the tips into hard nubs. "So you trust me enough to please you?"

"Oh...yeah."

"You trust me with your body?"

"Yes."

"Would you let me tie you up?"

She groaned. His roving hands made sitting still almost impossible. "Why would you want to do that?"

Curiosity combined with heat in his voice, causing her heart to flutter with a new set of nerves. He seemed to have no idea what kind of effect he had on her. Or maybe he did.

His tone turned even huskier. "You were the one who said that there're different kinds of trust. I just wondered how far you would go."

She had no idea how far she would go. She'd never acted this outrageously before. And yet her behavior with Quinn felt too good to be censored or inhibited.

His hands slowed, cupping her breasts, leaving her nipples aching for more attention. Concentrating on their conversation was such an effort. "If I agreed to let you tie me up, what would you do?"

"Whatever I wanted."

Whatever he wanted? Hadn't she already been letting him do whatever he wanted? But being tied up held other implications and insatiable need swept over her in a wave. To find out what else he intended, she'd have to agree. Heat pooled at her core, and she was learning that in this heightened state of arousal, not only were her defenses down, but her measure of trust had gone up. "Okay."

She'd just agreed to let him tie her up.

"You understand you'll be totally helpless and vulnerable. You'll be giving yourself up to me to do what I wish."

She shivered at the appeal of giving herself up to him. "Yes."

"And could you say that to me—if you didn't love me?"

She didn't want to go there. She didn't want to think. She wanted to stay embroiled in this erotic haze of need that was wrapped around them and kept her warm, willing. Wanton.

He nuzzled her ear, lifted her swollen breasts, flicking the tips with his thumbs.

"Quinn, I...can't think...when you do that."

"We need to change vehicles now." As if on cue, the carriage stopped. Quinn straightened her blouse and skirt, using the opportunity to run his hands over her breasts and hips and thighs.

He helped her from the carriage. And into a car? The seat was wide and made of leather. The sounds from the street faded as Quinn settled beside her and shut the door.

Immediately the vehicle began to move. And Quinn unbuttoned her blouse. "The driver?" Maggie asked.

''Can't see or hear us through the partition. And the windows are tinted. I will be able to see you— but no one else will.''

She didn't question that he had her protected from public view. She allowed him to help her remove her blouse and skirt. She kicked off her shoes. She was naked, sitting next to a fully dressed Quinn.

He scooped her up and lifted her onto his lap. Maggie tilted back her head, breathing in his scent. Before she realized what Quinn had done, he'd wedged his knees between her thighs and parted her legs.

He slipped something soft and silky over her wrists—tying her. She tugged, testing the bonds and found that she could move her wrists a few inches in any direction.

''Comfy?'' Quinn asked.

''Not exactly.''

''What's wrong?''

''Well, I'm sitting here open and ready and you aren't doing much of anything.''

He chuckled that rich sound that always riveted her. ''You're so impatient.''

Maggie desperately wanted his hands between her legs and on her breasts. Surely an hour had passed since her last orgasm. It seemed like forever. And yet Quinn wanted to nuzzle her ear and nip her neck.

It was then Maggie realized that while she was at his mercy, his erection beneath her bottom told her that he was just as turned on as she. And while he'd given her release several times, he'd had none. With that in mind, she wriggled her hips and her bottom, hoping to tease him and give just a little back of what he'd done to her.

"Maggie, if you keep squirming, I'm going to swat your bottom," Quinn promised.

Her heart skipped a beat and then kick started with a thump. "You wouldn't?"

"You couldn't stop me," he reminded her, his tone mild.

No way could he spank her butt while she was sitting on it. Maggie felt safe from his threat. Still, she was tied, naked, and Quinn didn't make idle threats. She stopped squirming.

That was when Quinn reached between her thighs and parted her folds, boldly taking hold of her clit between his thumb and finger. "No squirming, Maggie."

"You can't possibly expect me to…oh…hold still while you…ah…do that!"

"Well, just remember, I warned you what the consequences of squirming would be."

"Beast."

"Want me to stop?"

"No."

"I thought not."

She hadn't realized how hard it would be to hold still. Especially when she was already so sensitive that his lightest touch shot sizzling electricity through her. The worst part was never knowing if he intended to give her another orgasm, or if this time he would bring her just to the brink before he pulled back.

She tried to hold still. She did. But she was going to scream if he… "Quinn, please."

"Please, what?"

"Let me come."

"Sweet Maggie, are you sure?"

She whispered, "Please." She gripped the straps attached to her wrists and yanked, but they didn't budge. She tried to squeeze her legs together to press his fingers against her most sensitive places. But his knees kept her legs open.

She had to wait, and she bit her bottom lip in frustration.

"Would you like me inside you?" he asked, raising her hopes.

"Yes."

"Then you'll have to lean forward."

His hands on her bottom helped guide her up. Half crouched, legs wide. She waited for him to wrestle with his clothes. Heard the tearing of a condom. Then he was guiding her back onto his lap, his hand between her legs, his cock filling her completely. And like a wild woman she rode him, swiftly and steamily, rocking forward and back, using her legs to lift and lower herself.

And then she couldn't wait for him to catch up with her. She was exploding, teetering, her entire body tensing and releasing. And when she collapsed on Quinn's lap, sated, she realized that he was still hard inside her.

He breathed raggedly in her ear, his voice raw and edged with passion. "Maggie mine, you didn't even try to hold still."

"Are you complaining?"

"Nope." He sounded way too satisfied with himself. "I'm thinking how much fun I'm going to have heating up your bottom."

She swallowed hard, as, for the first time, the tiniest frisson of fear tightened her gut. "You don't mean that?"

"I do."

"Quinn, I'm not into pain."

He reached around and plucked at her nipple. "You know why you like this...because I'm drawing heat to a very sensitive area."

"But—"

She felt him lean forward and reach for something. She heard him twist off a bottle cap. More lotion?

And then he was spreading a liquid over her breasts, coating every inch of skin. "This oil has special properties."

At least he'd changed the subject from spankings. She most definitely wasn't into that. "You feel good."

She heard the whirring of an overhead panel sliding back. Air blew through the car. Cool air. But her breasts heated, the skin plumping, engorging. And she desperately needed his hands on her there.

She raised her voice to be heard above the rushing air. "What is that stuff?"

"Are you hot, Maggie?"

"Yes."

"The lotion was a warm-up for the oil. I'm going to slather this oil between your legs and over your bottom." He used his hands to tilt her up off his lap again. She had no choice but to lean forward and let him do as she wished.

He took his time, placing the oil on her hips, her cheeks, letting it drizzle between her buttocks, then cupping the excess between her thighs and rubbing there. Everywhere. He coated her folds, even slipped his slick fingers inside her for a moment, and when he pulled her back onto his lap, once again filling her with his cock, the sensation almost made her faint from the pleasure.

Wind whipped her hair, heated the oil on her skin, and she was squirming, frantic for him to let her move. But he held her still, trembling, one unmoving finger on her clit. All the blood in her veins, all the sensations seemed concentrated in her breasts, her bottom and between her thighs.

If he'd just move his finger, just once, she would come all over again. She'd never last another hour. Not when she was so ready to explode.

He urged her up again. Her legs trembled with the effort and with her need to take him again. The blaze between her thighs had her frantic to have him inside her.

"Stay there, Maggie."

And then he slapped her bottom. Once. Twice. Again. And again. She felt no pain. Just pure heat. And then she couldn't hold back, she came unglued, taking him into her, desperate to have him inside her. Without his strong hands guiding her hips, without him helping her wild gyrations, she might have fallen. Instead they came together, pure bright light searing through her, like a star going nova.

And afterward, when she collapsed onto him once more, she couldn't think. She couldn't move. She couldn't even rationalize what he'd done to her. She only knew that she'd never experienced such incredible pleasure. She hadn't known her body could do anything like that.

And when he lazily snaked his hand once again between her thighs, she thought she was ready to die from the joy he could generate. She hadn't the strength to summon up a word of protest. Like an empty rag doll, she was sure, he'd taken the stuffing out of her.

Nothing could top what they had just done, what she had just felt. Nothing. But when his fingers started moving again, she whimpered, sure that her heart couldn't recuperate. At least if she up and died, she'd go as a very satisfied woman.

QUINN SUPPOSED HE COULD have gone the noble route of holding back on sex to prove they shared more than lust together. But he saw no reason to deny themselves the connection of touching flesh to flesh and sharing the most intimate of acts.

At the same time, he wanted them both to have fun. Just because he hadn't experienced the kind of love a man has for a woman before now, didn't mean he couldn't recognize it when he felt it. When he began writing screenplays, he knew when he found the right word, knew when he visually portrayed the right emotion. No one had to tell him. No one had to verify he'd written a great screenplay—he just knew from the inside out. And when he put together the right script, director and cast, when all the elements fell into place, he didn't need an Academy Award to know he'd done good work. And he didn't need anyone to tell him that what he felt for Maggie was real and good and would last the rest of their lives. He knew.

Just as he understood that love needn't always be so serious. Love could also be light. Love included laughter, as well as the sharing of hopes and dreams. And he saw absolutely nothing wrong with mixing serious pleasure and deep conversation and good fun.

After the limo driver stopped, turned off the engine and headed to another vehicle to drive home, Quinn freed Maggie's hands, bundled her into a blanket and carried her along the windswept beach. She snuggled against him, completely trusting him to take her wherever he wanted.

Maggie's nose twitched. "Is that the ocean?"

"You'll soon see."

"I can hear the waves lapping on the shore."

She didn't protest that he carried her. She didn't once ask for him to set her down, just snuggled deeper against his chest.

Maggie loved him. Or she wouldn't have taken Laine's place.

Maggie loved him. Or she wouldn't have come here with him tonight. Nor would she have done what they had just done.

Maggie loved him—she just didn't know it yet. That's why she hadn't jumped all over the opportunity to open her own casting agency. She didn't want to take anything from him that could cloud the issue. Sweet, bold Maggie. Didn't she understand that she could have his love and her casting agency, too?

Quinn might have a reputation for ruthlessly going after what he wanted, but that he could also be patient was part of his key to success. If Maggie needed time to come to terms with her feelings, he would wait her out. And, meanwhile, they would work together, spend their nights together and watch the sun rise together.

Quinn had made arrangements earlier and everything looked perfect. "You can remove the blindfold."

Her fingers moved quickly, like a little kid eager to unwrap a present. It took her a moment and several blinks before her eyes focused on him. She didn't seem to care where he'd brought her. She only seemed interested in seeing his expression. He only hoped the firelight reflected the love in his eyes.

She reached up and placed her palm on his jaw. "Thank you."

"For what?"

She grinned. "For starters, giving me so many orgasms. And for arranging our night together."

"I'm going to give you so much that you'll be dying to grow old with me," he promised.

She stilled. Her eyes clouding with doubt.

He'd gone too far, too fast and left her behind. She wasn't ready to hear about forever. And he knew better, damn it.

To cover up his error in revealing too much, too soon, he spun in a circle, twirling her. Automatically she grabbed behind his neck to steady herself and when he cradled her as they fell to the blankets on the beach, she was breathless and laughing, her doubts set aside for now.

She craned her neck, taking in the campfire, the blanket and the custom trailer parked above the high-tide mark. Her eyebrow raised. "We're camping out?"

"In luxury. A wealthy friend owns two miles of this beach, so we're all alone. And that trailer has a bathroom with gold faucets and a marble tub big enough to fit two of us. There's a king-size mattress, and a gourmet meal, all cooked and waiting."

She settled back on the blanket and held out her arms to him. "We're spending the night here?"

He held up a finger, signaling he'd be with her in a moment. "You told me I could have all of Saturday night. I don't intend to waste a minute." He opened a huge basket and took out a thermos, two cups and a package of marshmallows. Per his instructions, long sticks had been included.

Maggie turned on her side on the blanket. The firelight caressed her skin and added red highlights to her blond hair. "How did you arrange all this?"

"I waved my magic director wand." One of the advantages of being a successful writer, director and producer was that not only could Quinn imagine how to set the scene, he could afford to follow through and indulge himself. "Shall I toast you a marshmallow?"

"Yes, please."

"You've been saying that a lot tonight." Enjoying the slight flare of her nostrils at his banter, he placed the marshmallow on the stick and held it over the fire.

"Just make sure you don't burn my marshmallow."

"Don't worry, I'll cook it to match my woman. Toasted golden brown on the outside and hot and melting on the inside."

Maggie tossed aside the blanket, laced her hands behind her head and wriggled as if she knew exactly how distracting she could be. Her full breasts with their tiny coral tips were the ultimate distraction—but no way was he going to overcook her marshmallow. At least that was the plan, until she snaked her hand into his lap and traced the rim of his cock right through his slacks.

"Is that what I am? Your woman?"

"I'd like you to be." He phrased his words with care, unwilling to frighten her again.

He turned the marshmallow over the flame, making sure to heat it evenly, and tried not to think about the sensations she was causing below the waist. It was too soon for him to harden fully, yet it was amazing what her teasing could do to his libido.

"So are we going to be mutually exclusive?"

Sheesh! What kind of a man did she think he was? One that could tell her he loved her, then skip off to see another woman? The value system he'd inherited from his parents might be different than what she'd gleaned from her more conservative midwest upbringing, but he didn't believe in that kind of behavior.

"Yes. We are going to be mutually exclusive." He frowned at her. "I don't believe in cheating, Maggie. I've seen too much of that kind of thing from my father. I love him and so did my mother, but he was always looking for someone who might love him more or better or differently. The truth is that he can't find a woman to love him as much as he loves himself.''

''And your mother?'' Maggie asked.

''She's so wrapped up in her work that she doesn't always have much to give at the end of the day. My father broke her heart and, although she tried three more times, I'm not sure she ever got over him.''

''You haven't had much of an example set for you.'' Maggie eyed the marshmallow and he blew on it to cool it for her. Burning her lips and mouth with anything less than his kisses wasn't what he had in mind.

''I learned early what I didn't want. It's not easy coming from the broken home of career oriented parents. I'm counting on you to teach me about the lasting part of love.'' Quinn tested the marshmallow's heat. ''Still too hot for you.''

Her eyes flickered with amusement. ''So I'm going to teach you about fidelity and you're going to decide what's too hot for me?''

''We'll each teach one another what we know best.'' He plucked the marshmallow off the stick and pulled it into two pieces. He could tell that she expected him to hand her half. Instead, he placed one half over each nipple.

''Ooh.''

''Too hot?''

''No.'' She giggled. ''But it sure is going to be fun when you're naked and it's my turn to toast one and place it on you.''

At that statement, his erection swelled to full proportions. And as for who was teaching whom about what was hot, Maggie could most certainly hold her own.

He suspected his eyes were full of hunger as the two marshmallow halves called to him.

"Well?" she prodded. "Aren't you going to lick me clean?"

"Eventually."

"What do you mean eventually? These marshmallows are cooling and sticky."

"Good. So they won't fall off."

"Why do I have to wait?" she asked, her beautiful lips pouting as he denied her immediate gratification in favor of prolonged anticipation.

"One tiny little marshmallow is not enough." He plucked another marshmallow out of the bag and pushed his stick through the center.

Maggie's eyes narrowed. Then she broke into a wide grin. "You go right ahead and toast your marshmallows, Quinn." She unzipped his zipper and ran the tip of her finger under the rim of his cock. "Take your time. I'm not in any hurry."

At her bold move, Quinn decided he could roast more than one marshmallow at a time. He placed two more on the stick before thrusting them over the flames.

"So what do you want out of our relationship?" she asked.

"Abundant sex. Monogamy. Companionship. Similar interests that don't compete with one another but enhance each other. Closeness. Help through troubled times.''

''Wow. That's quite a list.''

Quinn turned the marshmallow stick in his hand. ''I wasn't done. I want someone who cares about herself and others. Someone who takes care of herself and expects the same of me. In other words, I want you.''

''You mentioned sex first.''

''Sex is high on my priority list,'' he admitted. ''Especially with you.'' He stared into the flames. ''You know when you told me to prove that you loved me, I thought about all kinds of crazy things. Like trying to abstain while we got to know one another better.''

''And?'' she prodded.

''I didn't want to go that route.''

''Didn't want to deprive yourself?''

''That, too.'' He stood and let her pull off his pants and boxers, giving her free access to touch him wherever she pleased. ''But having sex with you is practically irresistible because I love the way you respond to me. It's how you always urge me further than I planned to go. And you're always open for a little experimentation.''

''And that's not lust because…?''

He hoped he wasn't going over the line again, scaring her with too much of the truth. ''Because I care about your enjoyment more than I do my own.''

13

QUINN CARED ABOUT HER enjoyment more than his own. At his words, Maggie's heart couldn't help softening another degree, even while her head issued warning bells. Quinn had begun his career as a writer. In his prodigious memory were embedded the perfect lines from a hundred screenplays which he could call upon when it suited him.

Did his words reflect his feelings? And if so, did caring about another person's pleasure more than his own mean that he had real feelings for her? Was that love? Maybe. But with Quinn it could also be ego. Part of his charm was that whatever he did, he did well. That included writing, directing and producing. That trait had shot him to the pinnacle of the Hollywood world before he was twenty-five. Polished, charming and well schooled in the art of keeping celebrities clamoring to be included in his life, he was a hard man to really know. Sometimes Maggie thought he was speaking from his heart, and other times he just seemed too damn polished to be real.

"Maggie." He checked his marshmallows for toasted perfection.

"Yes."

"You don't believe me. And making love isn't convincing you."

Was he reading her mind?

"So do you know what it's going to take?"

She had no idea.

"Time."

"Time?"

"Yes."

He tapped his temple with one finger. "Unfortunately it's impossible for you to crawl into my head and read my thoughts without me filtering them."

Maggie shifted on the blanket, listening intently. "And your point is?"

"You don't know what we've found together because we haven't been together—like this—for long enough."

She frowned at him, even as she fondled him. "You don't seem to have my doubts."

"I don't have *any* doubts. I'm sure about my feelings for you."

"Why?"

"Because I have faith in my ability to recognize that we fit together. Our bodies, our minds and our temperaments."

"You're telling me that love is a leap of faith?"

"Yes." He pulled the marshmallows away from the fire and planted the stick in the ground, allowing them to cool in the night air. "Falling in love is a risk." He grinned his most charming grin at her. "Love may be the greatest risk of all. And I'm finding the challenge exciting."

She loved that smile of his but wouldn't let him

charm her into automatically taking his words for the truth. "And when the challenge wears off?"

"I don't think it will. Not if we don't let it. The challenges may change in ways we can't anticipate— but that's what makes life interesting, don't you think?"

"I don't know." She didn't. Her head was spinning after all his philosophical mumbo jumbo. She'd tried to focus on his words, but as she watched him cool the marshmallows, she found her thoughts wandering to where he would put them. And she saw no reason why he should have all the fun. She held out her hand, palm up. "I want two of those, please."

"I'm more than willing to share." He pulled all three off the stick and handed her two.

Right before she placed one between her teeth, she demanded. "Kiss me, Quinn."

He leaned forward, his lips meeting hers as he took half the treat into his mouth. Feeding him like this made her warm all over. Or perhaps it was knowing that after he licked the sticky stuff off her lips, he'd move on to her breasts. And she still didn't know what he'd do with that leftover marshmallow, either, but she was up for every possibility.

Meanwhile, his kiss gave her ideas for the marshmallow she still had in her palm. She played and flattened the melted sugar until it was enlarged enough to wrap around the head of his jutting sex.

With his mouth still on hers, she could hear his swift intake of breath as she molded her hand to him, but he let her do as she pleased. And when she broke their kiss, she took her time nipping his neck, his powerful chest and his flat stomach on her way down to her intended target.

Maggie had never made love under the stars before. The sound of waves lapping gently on the beach was more sensual than any music. Her heart sang with joy and her body moved to a beat that was all Quinn's. She lost track of how many times they made love that night. How many times they gave one another pleasure.

But as they gazed over the Pacific, the sun rising at their backs in the morning, the orange streaks with ribbons of purple streaming over the water, she wondered if she'd ever before been this happy. Or if the feeling could possibly last.

Being with Quinn was special in so many ways. Right now, they were sitting holding hands in a comfortable silence, a blanket enveloping both of them. She was learning that she liked just being with him and cuddling with him in a hushed quiet, as much as she'd previously enjoyed their conversation.

Their lovemaking had been spectacular, involving all the senses. She adored touching and being touched. And Quinn's special male aroma alone could turn her on. So could his voice, which he used to provoke and arouse and push her further than she'd imagined possible. And never again would she see or taste a marshmallow without the treat being associated with the man.

But, most of all, she liked the way his mind worked. She'd always appreciated that he could out-think his competitors, but what she hadn't understood before was that his brilliance was part of a character that was kind, caring and giving—as well as arrogant, egotistical and eccentric at times.

"Quinn?"

"Yes."

"How come you don't think I changed places with Laine to get something from you?"

"I did at first." He squeezed her hand. "But then you never asked for anything."

She turned from the ocean to look into his eyes. She knew how much he'd always had difficulty trusting people because so many tried to use him to get ahead. Like finding their relative a job. Casting them in a part. Buying their screenplay. She'd even urged him to read Kimberly's, knowing her friend deserved a break, but that was how the business worked.

So she finally found the courage to ask him the question that was central to her believing his words about love. "By accepting the casting opportunity you offered, I will be taking from you. How do you know I love you—and not what you can do for me?"

"You taught me to answer that question."

"I did?" Maggie hadn't thought she could have taught Quinn anything. He always seemed ten steps ahead of her.

"If I lost my job tomorrow, would you still want to make love to me?"

"Of course. But you'd find another position within a day."

"Suppose my films all flopped and no one in Hollywood would hire me?"

"You'd still be wealthy."

"And if I lost everything in a string of failures? Would you still enjoy making love to me?"

"Yes. And you'd be back on top in no time, convincing new money men to back you."

"That's what you taught me."

"What? That there's someone who believes you'll always be a success? Or that there's someone out there who would believe in you even if you failed?"

"You're missing the point."

Maggie knew this issue was important but she just didn't get it. "You aren't being clear."

"What I'm saying is that you taught me that I can't separate Quinn the man from what I do for a living."

"O...kay." He was losing her here.

"When you grow up with parents as successful as mine, people fawn over you from an early age. I got cynical. And then I was an immediate success. So when I dated a woman, I always wondered if she would love me if I didn't come with wealth, power and status. You made me realize that's part of me. You can't separate me from what I do."

She cocked her head. "That's good, right?"

He chuckled and slung an arm over her shoulder. "Yes, Maggie, that's good."

"So you don't mind my nagging you to read Kimberly's script?" she teased.

He leaned over and nipped her ear, fanning a warm breath of desire down her neck. "I didn't say that."

She tried to shove him back, but he didn't budge. "Don't you dare try to distract me from the subject."

"Okay. I'll read it. But I'm not buying it if it's not any good—not even for you."

"QUINN. MAGGIE. ARE YOU dressed?" Kimberly's voice was followed by her appearance from behind the trailer.

"Hold up a minute," Quinn ordered, seemingly unfazed by his production assistant's sudden appearance.

He slid from beneath the blanket, and Maggie shivered as cold air replaced the warmth Quinn had lent her. He pulled on his slacks and slung a shirt over his shoulders, then turned to face Kimberly, his eyes curious, his face unreadable.

Maggie, her clothes nowhere in sight and nowhere as calm as Quinn, yanked the blanket to her chin. She already knew Kimberly wouldn't have tracked them to Canada and this beach if not for some emergency. Her heart started to pound like it did when her phone rang unexpectedly in the middle of the night.

"What's wrong?" Maggie asked.

Kimberly hurried to them, struggling to walk in heels over the rock-strewn beach and storm-tossed driftwood. Her eyes flitted, trying to avoid the campfire, the tumbled blankets, Quinn's bare chest and Maggie's shivers. Kimberly settled for looking at her feet and scowling at her ruined pumps.

Quinn frowned at Kimberly. "This had better be important or you—"

"Laine Lamonde and Dan O'Donnel have eloped." Kimberly thrust a piece of paper in Quinn's direction.

"Hmm," Maggie kept to herself the thought of how odd it was that Laine seemed to like short, balding men with large stomachs, like O'Donnel and her agent.

Kimberly handed him a sheet of paper. "Derek Parker faxed me this late last night."

"And Derek sent you to find us?" Maggie guessed, her thoughts racing, her stomach tensing with the magnitude of the news and how it would effect Quinn that Laine had married his competitor.

"Why?" Quinn was calm but Maggie had never seen him go so still. If he hadn't been spending all this time with her, he might have...what? If Laine had married Dan, there was likely nothing they could have done even if all their attention had been devoted to signing the star. Yet, Derek Parker might not see things that way.

Kimberly handed Quinn a cell phone. "Mr. Parker wants to speak with you."

Quinn glared at her. "I have a cell phone, and I turned it off. Do you know why?"

"Obviously you didn't want to be bothered." Kimberly kept her eyes downcast and Maggie felt sorry for her friend. Clearly, she'd not wanted to come here, but she couldn't very well have ignored such a request without losing her job.

"Hey, don't shoot the messenger," Maggie told Quinn gently, wishing she could think of something to help him.

Quinn grunted and took the cell phone. He walked down the beach out of earshot to make his call, leaving Maggie and Kimberly alone. Maggie sighed. "This may be my fault."

"That Laine married Dan O'Donnel?" Kimberly

kicked off her shoes and settled onto a corner of the blanket. "Oh, yeah. That must be all your fault."

"No. That Quinn turned off his phone." Maggie sighed. "Quinn agreed to read your script."

"Yeah, right."

"This time, he meant it."

"Oh, Maggie." Kimberly threw her arms around her. "You shouldn't have asked him again. Not when you're…when you two are…"

"Together?" Maggie finished for her obviously embarrassed friend. "He wants me to cast his next movie, too."

"That's wonderful," Kimberly's voice rose with genuine enthusiasm.

Maggie wished she could share Kimberly's excitement. She picked at the blanket, and her eyes followed Quinn down the beach. She didn't like him taking heat for spending time with her instead of taking care of business. The man was entitled to a life, wasn't he? However, studio people expected their employees to eat, bathe and make love with their cell phones handy. Parker wouldn't be pleased that Quinn had deliberately put himself out of touch—especially during a crisis of this magnitude.

Maggie tried to explain her gloomy mood to Kimberly, who was not aware of the hoops the studios made Quinn jump through to secure financial support for his films. "I don't feel good about accepting Quinn's offer when he may have just lost major funding for his picture."

"Why would he lose funding?" Kimberly asked.

Sometimes Maggie forgot how much Kimberly still

had to learn about the business. "Because Parker intends to back whoever signs Laine. He feels her American debut will assure the film's success. Without Laine, Quinn won't have the money for the costumes and set that are so necessary—"

"Got it." Kimberly stared at her, thinking hard. "Did Quinn really offer to let you cast—"

"Yes. But there might not even be a movie now." Miserable over the sudden turn of events, Maggie's eyes went to Quinn. He strode toward them, his legs eating up large chunks of sand with every step. He looked energized, ready to do battle and take on the world. She should have known Quinn would come up with a new plan to save the film and her hopes escalated.

"You impersonated Laine once—maybe you could play her part," Kimberly suggested.

Maggie rolled her eyes at the sky. "Thanks, but Laine is gorgeous. And I'm not an actress—I'm a casting director."

The wind must have carried some of their conversation to the approaching Quinn. He leaned toward Maggie and tipped up her chin, then kissed her lightly on the lips. "You're going to do what you do best, Maggie."

Taken aback that he'd kissed her right in front of Kimberly, Maggie was having trouble concentrating on his words. What did she do best? Surely he wasn't referring to the marshmallows? Heat rose up her neck. "Huh?"

"You're going to cast me a new leading lady."

Quinn's eyes twinkled. "Someone so fantastic that Parker will need to have me sign her right away."

"But he wants Laine," Maggie said, her thoughts still fuzzy from lack of sleep, hours of lovemaking and Quinn's latest kiss. Apparently he had no intention of hiding his feelings for her. She didn't know why she'd thought he might, hadn't actually thought about facing their friends and associates until that moment, but she was glad that Quinn had made their kiss so easy and normal and open.

Quinn's mouth turned up in a cocky grin. "He's no longer fixated on Laine Lamonde."

Maggie didn't pay too much attention to Quinn's statement. Her mind was sifting through her memory to Quinn's conversation with Laine. She remembered and could feel her hopes brightening. "Didn't you tell Laine that Julia Roberts was interested in the part?"

Quinn shook his head. "That was simply a bluff to make Laine more eager to sign with us."

"Then how did you manage to change Parker's mind?" Maggie asked, fascinated by how vibrant Quinn could be after making love to her all night. He still looked ready to take on the world.

"Laine is relatively unknown in the U.S., but she is a European star," Quinn continued, "and I convinced him that the current hot trend is to take an unknown and build them into a megastar."

Maggie hoped he was right but she wasn't sold. "I don't know, Quinn. The reason stars are paid the big bucks is that people come to see them even if they know nothing about the film."

Kimberly was grinning. "An unknown can create

stellar publicity exactly because no one knows anything about them. Everyone would want a piece of them, their background, their past lovers. Think about when Vivian Leigh was cast in *Gone With the Wind*. And the American public loves rags-to-riches stories.''

''Like America's fascination with the show *American Idol?*'' Maggie asked, suddenly understanding the brilliance of Quinn's concept. Talk about turning lemons into lemonade—he should be crowned the lemonade king.

''Exactly how I sold Parker on Maggie's new sensation,'' Quinn agreed.

''Maggie has a new sensation?'' Kimberly's eyes were lit with curiosity.

Maggie turned her head from Kimberly to Quinn, her pulse now leaping. ''What new sensation?''

Quinn chuckled. ''I have no idea, but you've got twenty-four hours to find her. Parker wants to see her screen test on Monday morning.''

TO MAGGIE, THE TRIP BACK to L.A. was a blur of phone calls, meetings and full-fledged panic. What had ever made her decide she could cast a movie? Especially on such short notice?

Usually major stars came attached to a project and the casting agency was responsible for finding the supporting characters, the walk-ons, etc. But she had to start from scratch. At least she'd already read the script. But the moment she returned to L.A., she had to hit the ground running.

In the middle of the storm, Quinn took charge of

arranging for the offices, equipment and temporary personnel that she'd need for her casting agency within Simitar Studios. By the time they arrived at the private airport and drove straight to the studio, Maggie felt numb from lack of sleep and disappointment. She'd already called the agents of her first three choices at their homes on Sunday—not making her the most popular woman in town. Two of the actresses were already tied up contractually by other projects and the third was five months pregnant and taking a two-year maternity leave.

Despite her worry, the office Quinn arranged for her took her breath away. She had two windows, a series of filing cabinets and a superfast computer system connection. Quinn had even arranged for two temps to work through the night. She now had sandwiches and coffee, a bowl of fruit, a working phone system, a private media room filled with VCR equipment to watch tapes of actresses. And he'd copied his "contact" file from his PDA right into her computer. So she also had the phone numbers, business and private, of practically everyone in Hollywood.

That Quinn could have accomplished so much by making a few phones calls shouldn't have astounded her. She'd seen him work this kind of magic before. But never had all his efforts been on *her* behalf— well, not unless she counted Saturday night. But this was different. This was business. And she wanted to throw her arms around his neck and plant kisses on his cheeks to thank him.

But he'd left her to get organized for her search. And the best way to thank Quinn was to come up with someone dynamite. Kimberly flopped into a chair opposite Maggie in her new office. Her friend seemed just as stunned by the sudden change in Maggie's responsibilities as Maggie.

"What can I do to help?" Kimberly asked as she shoved a cup of coffee in Maggie's direction.

Maggie sipped the drink, appreciating the rich flavor. "I've been thinking that we need to go with someone unknown to the public."

"We don't have time to start canvassing every agent in town."

Maggie appreciated the "we." Kimberly was ready to stay here with her and work through the night to help. And she had yet to ask one question about finding Maggie and Quinn together on the beach—although, knowing Kimberly, curiosity must be eating at her. Right from their first meeting, Maggie had appreciated Kimberly's intelligence, her wit and her loyalty. With their mutual interest in the film industry, their office acquaintance had blossomed into many nights of fun where they'd seen movies and plays and… *The play*. The play she and Kimberly had missed last week gave her an idea.

Maggie grinned. "Kimberly, what about Serena Kendall?"

"The UCLA actress? She would be brilliant, but she has no experience in front of the cameras. She's a stage actress, albeit with all the right qualities."

"So we get her a good coach."

"Lots of actors make the transition from stage to film, but it can take years."

"We don't have years. In fact, we have until tomorrow morning when she'll have to do a screen test. I wonder if she has an agent? No matter. We'll find her one.'' Maggie picked up her purse. ''Come on. We're going to UCLA.''

Kimberly followed her out the door. ''I'm right behind you, but what is Quinn going to say about you hiring a complete unknown?''

''He said he trusts my judgment,'' Maggie told Kimberly, yet she knew Quinn was counting on her to find an experienced actress. However, the A-list stars were unavailable and Maggie had always had a feeling about Serena. She'd seen her act twice before. Once she'd played an innocent girl and in another play she'd been bold, sassy and strong.

Finding Serena proved easy enough. The drama student was listed in the campus directory and her roommate told them they could find her waiting tables at a nearby pizzeria.

As soon as they walked in, the heavenly aroma of pizza hit them, yeasty dough and garlicky tomato sauce. But they didn't have time to eat. Maggie spotted the waitress. ''Over there.''

Without makeup, her face was stunning. Serena's skin was clear, her nose straight, her teeth white and perfect. She walked smoothly between the tables, a pitcher of beer in one hand, a tray of iced mugs in the other.

Maggie stepped in her path and introduced herself. ''Serena Kendall, I'm Maggie Miller and I'd like a moment of your time.''

Serena didn't have a chance to respond before Kimberly plucked the pitcher of beer out of the waitress's hands and delivered it herself. Maggie took Serena's arm and led her to a booth. "I've seen you on stage and liked your work."

Serena's full mouth widened into a friendly grin. "Thanks." She glanced at Kimberly, who was frowning at the impatient college boys at Serena's table. "But I really should get back to work."

"I'm casting a movie and I think you'd be perfect for a part."

"Is this a porn film because—"

"You ever heard of Quinn Scott?"

"Quinn Scott?" Serena's elegant brow lifted in either puzzlement or disbelief.

"You have heard of him?" *Please,* Maggie prayed, *don't let Serena be an airhead.* Maggie didn't have time to coddle the kid. She had to be a professional.

"Everyone's heard of Quinn Scott." Serena sucked in her breath. Then she pinched her arm. "Ow. I guess I'm not dreaming, huh?"

"Look, I'm not promising you anything, but we have to get you ready for a screen test first thing in the morning."

"Do you have a business card?"

Obviously Serena was skeptical, and levelheaded, which would stand her in good stead in this business. Maggie silently thanked Quinn for his ability to anticipate her needs. She dug into her purse and gave out her first business card.

She pressed it into Serena's hand. "Have you ever worked in front of a camera?"

"I did TV commercials as a kid."

"Great." She'd had a feeling Serena would be perfect and Maggie's confidence rose another two notches. She fished five pages of dialogue from her purse and handed them over. "How fast can you memorize this?"

"I practically have a photographic memory." Maggie couldn't believe her luck. If Serena was telling the truth, she had not only brains and talent but she wouldn't forget her lines, either. She looked at the expression on the young woman's face. Although Serena looked less skeptical, she still seemed baffled. Maggie couldn't exactly blame her. After all, it wasn't every day that a casting agent walked up to a waitress and told her she had a chance to be a star. "Maggie, why all the rush?"

"Laine Lamonde was going to star in this movie, but she eloped. To secure the financing we need, we have to replace her immed—"

"Did you say *star?*" Serena's lovely peach complexion turned green. And then Maggie's perfect candidate fainted.

14

"KIMBERLY!" MAGGIE CAUGHT the fainting Serena in her arms, but the unconscious weight had her staggering. "Help."

Within moments, Kimberly, followed by the trio of beer drinkers that she'd just served, had lowered Serena into a booth. Maggie dipped the corner of a napkin into a glass of ice water and bathed Serena's neck.

"What happened? I swear, Maggie, every time I leave you alone you are—"

"Hush." Maggie gazed down at Serena's eyes, which were fluttering. "She's about to wake up and I don't need you scaring—"

"I'd say you already did that without my help." Kimberly leaned into the booth and helped Maggie prop up the woozy Serena. "Show's over, guys. But thanks for the help."

Serena stared at Maggie. "Are you for real?"

Maggie chuckled from a combination of nerves and the realization that Quinn had made her important enough to cause a young woman to faint. Her change in status was so sudden she hadn't taken in all the ramifications yet. However, she'd been around the movie industry long enough to know that people who had once snubbed her as a mere assistant would now try and curry her favor. No doubt other secretaries in the company would learn that Maggie and Quinn were together. They'd assume he'd promoted her because of that and look down on her for it. Success always came with a price, and if it included dealing with fainting young women, then Maggie would learn to cope. Perhaps she should have been more subtle.

But the damage was done. Serena knew that Maggie wanted her to star in the film. "Perhaps I shouldn't have told you how important the part is until after your screen test. But if you can't hold up to the pressure, it's best that we know now."

Serena sipped water from the glass Kimberly held to her lips. She swallowed, then lifted her chin and squared her delicate shoulders. "I'll be fine. I won't let you down," Serena glanced at the business card still clutched in her hand, "Ms. Miller."

"Call me Maggie. I don't want to intimidate you and have you faint on me again. Next time I might not catch you and I don't want you reading for that part with a bloody nose or a black eye."

"Don't worry. I'll be brilliant—if I don't faint." Serena dipped her fingers in the glass and splashed drops of water over her face.

Kimberly frowned at her. "You aren't pregnant, are you?"

Maggie should have thought of asking the girl that and held her breath as she waited for the answer.

"Not a chance." Serena shook her head. "Men seem to prefer to admire me from afar."

Serena explained the situation to the manager who immediately offered to work her tables for her and then wished her good luck. Then Maggie and Kimberly whisked the girl out of the pizzeria. During the car ride back to the studio, Serena read over the pages while Maggie woke up a makeup artist, a stylist, a set designer, a costume consultant, an acting coach, a cameraman and a photographer and asked them to meet back at the studio. She was determined to oversee every detail of the screen test to show off her "sensation" to the best of their ability.

"Who's going to read opposite me?" Serena asked. "It sure would help to practice with whoever he is."

Maggie hadn't thought that far ahead. She'd been so busy trying to replace Laine, she hadn't yet thought about the costar. Maggie looked at Kimberly, who shrugged.

"We'll find someone," Maggie told her.

"What about Quinn?" Kimberly suggested.

Maggie recalled Laine's request. Three men would play opposite the female lead, and the oldest man would be a perfect role for Quinn's father. "How about Jason Scott?"

"Oh, my God. You want me to do my screen test with Jason Scott?"

"Don't you dare faint again," Maggie warned her.

"Hey, a man like that knows how to make you look good," Kimberly told her.

"A man like Jason Scott knows how to steal the scene," Serena countered.

"Just read the script." Maggie flipped open her cell phone and filled Quinn in on the situation, then asked,

"What do you think about asking your father to read opposite our new sensation?"

"Your new what?" Serena paled again.

Maggie sighed and Kimberly rolled her eyes at the ceiling. Then bless her, Kimberly distracted Serena so Maggie could finish her conversation with Quinn.

"Maggie, I'm not sure I want you to meet my father," Quinn's tone was light.

Maggie wondered if Quinn was ashamed of her, or having second thoughts about his claim to love her. Meeting his family would make that awkward—especially if he'd lied to her.

Confidence, Maggie. Quinn's not a liar.

"Why don't you want me to meet your father?"

"Because he's afraid you'll fall in love with me." Maggie almost dropped the phone at the sound of Jason Scott's voice on the same line. Quinn must have made it a conference call. She would have recognized Jason's famous voice anywhere.

"Get over yourself, Dad. You aren't that gorgeous."

"Sure he is." Maggie disagreed, causing the older actor to chuckle.

"I wasn't ready for you to meet because I knew you two would gang up on me," Quinn teased. "So, Dad, you willing to help out a pretty young girl with her first screen test?"

"Hmm. Is she the one who made you miss our weekly breakfast?" Jason asked, and from the sound of his voice, Maggie knew he was joking. Obviously Jason already knew about Maggie. And she couldn't help wondering what Quinn had told his father about her.

As if she wouldn't have enough riding on this screen test, now she also had to worry about the impression she might make on Jason, Quinn's father. Under normal circumstances, meeting such a megastar wouldn't have thrown her. But this was Jason Scott. All through her childhood, she'd considered several men industry icons. Harrison Ford. Sean Connery. And Jason Scott.

"Dad, you can flirt with the actress all you want—even if she's too young to be your daughter. But don't mess with my casting director or I'll tell everyone that you need Viagra."

"I do not." Jason sounded indignant.

Maggie stepped in to soothe ruffled feathers. "Sir, we would consider it an honor if you would help Serena through her screen test. She's a bit nervous and no doubt could benefit from your experience."

Had she laid it on too thick? Quinn chuckled. And then Jason did, too. "Ah, this Maggie knows how to handle men. I should have known you'd pick a good one."

"Does that mean yes?" Maggie asked.

"Honey—"

"Dad, don't flirt with my woman." Quinn put a little steel into his tone, but Maggie caught the teasing in it, too. She'd also heard his admission to his father that Maggie was "his woman" and a warm thrill went through her at the words. Quinn certainly wasn't shy about his feelings or about staking his territory.

"Touchy, isn't he?" Jason asked, but his question

was rhetorical. "Maggie, honey." He used the endearment again, totally ignoring Quinn's admonition. "I can't wait to meet you."

TALK ABOUT PRESSURE. Maggie felt as if her entire life was coming down to Monday morning's screen test. Serena was dressed and finished with the makeup artist and stylist by seven. She'd had her lines down pat for hours and the acting coach was giving her last-minute directions.

Jason had even arrived early and done several runthroughs, charming all of the ladies and enjoying himself immensely. Maggie, however, had yet to meet him. She'd been busy making sure of last-minute details. Though she was the casting director, she still had the job of Quinn's assistant. The caffeine-free, special blend of coffee that Derek Parker preferred along with his favorite chocolate chip cookies were nearby. And she'd printed up glossy photos of Serena with a list of her acting credits for Derek to peruse. Normally a man of his stature didn't actually watch the screen test but waited in his office for film to be sent up. But with millions of dollars riding on this decision, he'd made it a point to announce he would be there for the screen test.

Quinn strode into Maggie's office and handed her a long-stemmed rose. He brushed her cheek with his lips, then eased her to her feet and hugged her. "Did you sleep at all?"

She shook her head. "I tried."

"You must be exhausted."

"I'm running on pure adrenaline."

Quinn cupped her under the chin and smoothed her cheek with his thumb. "Maggie, Maggie, Maggie. It's only a movie."

"Making movies is what you do. And you're good at it. I don't want to let you down."

"You won't. However, Derek Parker may have his own ideas about whether or not Serena is any good. Either way...I'll still love you."

"Quinn, you really need that silver tongue of yours to stop—"

"That's not what you said back on the beach."

"—saying the most perfect lines."

"Why?" he demanded.

"Because I'll expect you to keep on saying them."

"Darling, I don't see that we have a problem here. Do you think I'm going to run out of good lines?"

Irrationally, she was afraid the moment she told him that she loved him he was going to run out on her. Although she knew that Quinn could commit to his career, the idea of him committing to a person, to her, seemed too good to be true. And Maggie was afraid to believe in happily-ever-after.

However, she loved him. She could admit that to herself now. She wasn't exactly sure when she'd fallen in love with him, probably way before she'd decided to take Laine Lamonde's place. But that love had been one of friendship and infatuation. Since she'd gotten to know Quinn better, her feelings had deepened, rocking her, rolling through her, with a ripping passion that scared her.

And what scared her even more was that she knew how much Quinn liked his challenges. If she told him what he wanted to hear, would his feelings lessen? Would his interest dwindle? She supposed there was only one way to find out, but the words clogged in her throat.

"What's wrong?"

She wiped away a stray tear. "I've got something in my eye."

"Maggie, Serena is going to be brilliant. And Derek's going to be so impressed he'll be begging us to let him finance the film."

How could she not love this man? He hadn't even seen Serena, but he believed in Maggie. His confidence was in the angle of his stubborn chin, in the lilt of his voice and in the glint in his eyes. And that confidence encompassed everything he did, the way he worked full speed, the way he played, the way he would try anything once. The way he loved—full-out.

She took his hands between her own. "I love you, Quinn."

"About damn time you realized that." His eyes glinted with amusement and pleasure, then his mouth joined hers.

That's how Derek Parker and Jason Scott found them—entwined in each other's arms. At the interruption, Maggie would have pulled back, but Quinn held her there, finishing his kiss with the same thoroughness he finished every task. And finally when he was good and ready, and Maggie was dying a little inside with embarrassment, Quinn released her mouth and then placed a protective arm over Maggie's shoulder. "Maggie, you already know Derek Parker."

She held out her hand and shook his.

"And my father, Jason."

Jason bypassed a handshake for a hug, a careful hug, which didn't smear his makeup or mess up his immaculately combed hair, while Quinn pretended to be jealous. She could see from the shared looks between father and son that they were close. Before anyone had a chance to say more, Kimberly's voice came in over the intercom. "We're all set down here."

"We're coming."

The screening room was dark and the set well lit and empty as everyone took their seats. Jason had gone backstage and Maggie ended up sitting between Derek and Quinn. She held Quinn's hand tightly as a grip moved a light. Then Serena and Jason walked onto the set and took their places.

Quinn leaned over and whispered in Maggie's ear. "Serena has a fresh look to her, and skin and cheekbones that the camera will love. If she can act—"

"She can act." Maggie assured him.

"Does she mind taking her clothes off?" Quinn asked.

Maggie dug her elbow into his side. "I tell you I love you and within an hour you're asking me to get another woman to take off her clothes for you?"

"Serena would have to do nude love scenes in Kimberly's movie."

"Kimberly's movie?" Maggie looked at him in confusion. "You read the script?"

"It's very good. With a few erotic love scenes, it could be great. Of course, I'll need Kimberly to authenticate those scenes. You think Serena would object to nudity?"

"I don't know." Maggie's thoughts were spinning. Quinn had read Kimberly's script and he'd liked it enough to think about who should play the lead. She couldn't wait to tell Kimberly and hoped her friend was up for verifying the script to meet Quinn's exacting standards. But, most of all, she wanted to kiss Quinn for being so wonderful.

And then the lights dimmed and Serena and Jason fell into their roles. Watching the transition was like magic. Jason shed his own persona like an old coat. One moment he was Quinn's father, and the next, he took on the demeanor of the man he was portraying. His shoulders slumped, just a little, and he moved with the hesitation of someone unsure of himself.

And Serena straightened. She grew bolder before their eyes, displaying the acting ability that Maggie remembered from seeing her on stage. Only this time her movements weren't as exaggerated. She'd toned down her performance for film where the camera's closeups would reveal the tiniest expressions.

Maggie held her breath. She didn't once look at Quinn or Derek to see what they thought. The performance took on a life of its own and the magic they created sparkled with chemistry.

Maggie didn't need Quinn and Derek to tell her that the scene worked on levels she didn't understand. She only knew her heart went out to the gentleman Jason had become while she only felt sympathy for the younger woman who was rejecting him. Serena was gracious and brazen and so full of life Maggie couldn't help but wish her well.

They did the scene in one take. When the director

said, "Cut," and the lights came back on, Maggie wanted to leap up and do a victory dance. But instead she forced herself to look at Quinn. He signaled her with a thumbs-up.

Derek shook Quinn's hand. "If she looks as good on film as on the stage, we're set to go."

Maggie sank back into her chair. Her palms damp with sweat, her pulse racing, she had no idea how Quinn could stay so calm when she felt like jumping out of her skin and racing around the room.

Quinn walked Derek to the door then returned to Maggie. "Serena's going to be a big star, Maggie, and she'll owe a lot of that to you for discovering her."

"Thank you, Quinn. I couldn't have discovered her if you hadn't given me this chance." Maggie lifted the seat's arm between them and snuggled against him, pleased that he'd believed in her right from the start. She liked being with Quinn. Liked how she felt about herself when she was with him.

"I'm only disappointed in one thing." Quinn stroked her arm lazily.

He was disappointed? How could he be disappointed when Maggie was bubbling with happiness? What had she missed? "You're disappointed?"

"Our weekend in Vancouver was cut short. So I think we should pack several bags to take to Tahiti."

"Tahiti?" Maggie stiffened.

"Not even Kimberly will find us in Tahiti."

"What are you talking about?"

"I always thought one of those huts in Mooréa that

juts out over the water would be the perfect place for a honeymoon.''

"Honeymoon?'' *Oh, God.* "To have a honeymoon, you have to get married.''

"Okay.''

"What do you mean, okay?''

"Well, didn't you just propose to me?'' His voice was full of laughter.

"I didn't.''

"But you want to marry me because you love me, right?''

"I haven't even thought about—''

"Don't worry, darling, I'll handle everything. I'll arrange the tickets. I'll do the packing. And I'll bring *lots* of marshmallows.''

Epilogue

IN TYPICAL QUINN FASHION the wedding was extravagant, lavish and elegant. Since Maggie had been swamped with casting Quinn's next movie, all she'd had to do was go to a dress fitting and show up for the ceremony. Quinn had sent over makeup artists, stylists and jewelry consultants. He'd hired a wedding planner to take care of the myriad of details, so the weeks leading up to the wedding hadn't quite prepared Maggie for the extravaganza of over a thousand guests, a sumptuous sit-down dinner and the press, who'd been threatened to behave or face eviction.

During the ceremony, Maggie gazed into Quinn's loving eyes and wondered how she'd gotten so lucky. Getting her lines right as she said her vows was difficult since every time she glanced at her handsome husband she went a little breathless. Quinn in black tie and tux was almost as yummy as Quinn without any clothes at all. She ached to be in his arms, alone with him, and her desire must have shown on her face.

After the ceremony, he leaned over and whispered, "Just a little longer, Maggie darling, and then you'll be all mine."

Then friends and family surrounded the happy couple. Kimberly found Maggie and hugged her tight. Her friend looked fabulous in the emerald gown and sparkling necklace Quinn had picked out for the maid of honor.

Kimberly chuckled. "You're glowing, Maggie."

"It's Quinn's doing."

Kimberly shook her head, her grin wide. "You went after what you wanted and now you're reaping the rewards. You have a great time in Tahiti, okay?"

"And you enjoy Europe." Quinn was sending Kimberly to Great Britain to verify every scene in her screenplay. When she succeeded, Quinn would back, direct and produce Kimberly's film.

"I will." Kimberly sounded merry but Maggie caught a hint of worry that her friend couldn't quite hide.

"What?"

"Did you know Quinn added love scenes that I'm supposed to verify?"

Quinn chuckled. "You better bring a friend over there with you. A good one."

Kimberly nodded but Maggie knew she didn't have a man in her life at the moment. She made a mental note to call her friend from Tahiti—and then a crowd of well-wishers separated Kimberly from Quinn and Maggie.

Hours later, after dancing and posing for pictures, Maggie and Quinn departed in a limousine for the private jet that would fly them to the South Pacific. The plane sported a master suite and a king-size bed. Maggie wouldn't have to wait until they reached the turquoise waters and powdery beaches of Tahiti to seduce her new husband.

Quinn placed an arm over her shoulder. "What's the most gorgeous bride in the world thinking?"

"About joining the mile-high club."

"Maggie darling. I do believe your interest in me is bordering on obsession."

"That's what I love about you, Quinn."

"What?"

"You're so humble."

"Humble enough to tell you I'm obsessed with you, too."

"Then it's mutual." Maggie raised her lips to his. "Now shut up and kiss me."

HARLEQUIN® Blaze™

USA TODAY bestselling author
Julie Kenner
started it all with a few
SILENT CONFESSIONS

But what happens once those
whispered words are put into *action?*

Find out in:

SILENT DESIRES
by Julie Kenner
August 2003

Lately erotic bookstore clerk Joan Bennetti
has been reading more naughty books than she sells.
And she's starting to get a few ideas of her own....

Don't miss the fireworks!

Look for it wherever Harlequin books are sold.

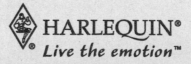

HARLEQUIN®
Live the emotion™

Visit us at www.eHarlequin.com

HBSDR

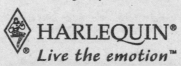

HARLEQUIN®
Temptation.

*Legend has it that
the only thing that can bring down a Quinn
is a woman...*

Now we get to see for ourselves!

The youngest Quinn brothers have grown up.
They're smart, they're sexy...and they're about to be
brought to their knees by their one true love.

Don't miss the last three books in
Kate Hoffmann's dynamic miniseries...

The Mighty Quinns

Watch for:
THE MIGHTY QUINNS: LIAM
(July 2003)

THE MIGHTY QUINNS: BRIAN
(August 2003)

THE MIGHTY QUINNS: SEAN
(September 2003)

Available wherever Harlequin books are sold.

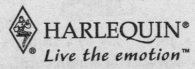

HARLEQUIN®
Live the emotion™

Visit us at www.eHarlequin.com

HTMQ

Is your man too good to be true?

Hot, gorgeous AND romantic?
If so, he could be a Harlequin® Blaze™ series cover model!

Our grand-prize winners will receive a trip for two to New York City to
shoot the cover of a Blaze novel, and will stay at the luxurious Plaza Hotel.
Plus, they'll receive $500 U.S. spending money!
The runner-up winners will receive $200 U.S.
to spend on a romantic dinner for two.

It's easy to enter!

In 100 words or less, tell us what makes your boyfriend or spouse a true romantic
and the perfect candidate for the cover of a Blaze novel, and include in your submission
two photos of this potential cover model.

All entries must include the written submission of the contest entrant, two photographs of the model
candidate and the Official Entry Form and Publicity Release forms completed in full and signed by
both the model candidate and the contest entrant. Harlequin, along with the experts at
Elite Model Management, will select a winner.

For photo and complete Contest details, please refer to the Official Rules on the next page. All entries
will become the property of Harlequin Enterprises Ltd. and are not returnable.

**Please visit www.blazecovermodel.com to download a copy of the Official Entry Form and
Publicity Release Form or send a request to one of the addresses below.**

Please mail your entry to: **Harlequin Blaze Cover Model Search**

In U.S.A.
P.O. Box 9069
Buffalo, NY
14269-9069

In Canada
P.O. Box 637
Fort Erie, ON
L2A 5X3

No purchase necessary. Contest open to Canadian and U.S. residents who are 18 and over.
Void where prohibited. Contest closes September 30, 2003.

HBCVRMODEL1

HARLEQUIN BLAZE COVER MODEL SEARCH CONTEST 3569 OFFICIAL RULES
NO PURCHASE NECESSARY TO ENTER

1. To enter, submit two (2) 4" x 6" photographs of a boyfriend or spouse (who must be 18 years of age or older) taken no later than three (3) months from the time of entry: a close-up, waist up, shirtless photograph; and a fully clothed, full-length photograph, then, tell us, in 100 words or fewer, why he should be a Harlequin Blaze cover model and how he is romantic. Your complete "entry" must include: (i) your essay, (ii) the Official Entry Form and Publicity Release Form printed below completed and signed by you (as "Entrant"), (iii) the photographs (with your hand-written name, address and phone number, and your model's name, address and phone number on the back of each photograph), and (iv) the Publicity Release Form and Photograph Representation Form printed below completed and signed by your model (as "Model"), and should be sent via first-class mail to either: Harlequin Blaze Cover Model Search Contest 3569, P.O. Box 9069, Buffalo, NY, 14269-9069, or Harlequin Blaze Cover Model Search Contest 3569, P.O. Box 637, Fort Erie, Ontario L2A 5X3. All submissions must be in English and be received no later than September 30, 2003. Limit: one entry per person, household or organization. **Purchase or acceptance of a product offer does not improve your chances of winning.** All entry requirements must be strictly adhered to for eligibility and to ensure fairness among entries.

2. Ten (10) Finalist submissions (photographs and essays) will be selected by a panel of judges consisting of members of the Harlequin editorial, marketing and public relations staff, as well as a representative from Elite Model Management (Toronto) Inc., based on the following criteria:

Aptness/Appropriateness of submitted photographs for a Harlequin Blaze cover—70%
Originality of Essay—20%
Sincerity of Essay—10%

In the event of a tie, duplicate finalists will be selected. The photographs submitted by finalists will be posted on the Harlequin website no later than November 15, 2003 (at www.blazecovermodel.com), and viewers may vote, in rank order, on their favorite(s) to assist in the panel of judges' final determination of the Grand Prize and Runner-up winning entries based on the above judging criteria. All decisions of the judges are final.

3. All entries become the property of Harlequin Enterprises Ltd. and none will be returned. Any entry may be used for future promotional purposes. Elite Model Management (Toronto) Inc. and/or its partners, subsidiaries and affiliates operating as "Elite Model Management" will have access to all entries including all personal information, and may contact any Entrant and/or Model in its sole discretion for their own business purposes. Harlequin and Elite Model Management (Toronto) Inc. are separate entities with no legal association or partnership whatsoever having no power to bind or obligate the other or create any expressed or implied obligation or responsibility on behalf of the other, such that Harlequin shall not be responsible in any way for any acts or omissions of Elite Model Management (Toronto) Inc. or its partners, subsidiaries and affiliates in connection with the Contest or otherwise and Elite Model Management shall not be responsible in any way for any acts or omissions of Harlequin or its partners, subsidiaries and affiliates in connection with the contest or otherwise.

4. All Entrants and Models must be residents of the U.S. or Canada, be 18 years of age or older, and have no prior criminal convictions. The contest is not open to any Model that is a professional model and/actor in any capacity at the time of the entry. Contest void wherever prohibited by law; all applicable laws and regulations apply. Any litigation within the Province of Quebec regarding the conduct or organization of a publicity contest may be submitted to the Régie des alcools, des courses et des jeux for a ruling, and any litigation regarding the awarding of a prize may be submitted to the Régie only for the purpose of helping the parties reach a settlement. Employees and immediate family members of Harlequin Enterprises Ltd., D.L. Blair, Inc., Elite Model Management (Toronto) Inc. and their parents, affiliates, subsidiaries and all other agencies, entities and persons connected with the use, marketing or conduct of this Contest are not eligible to enter. Acceptance of any prize offered constitutes permission to use Entrants' and Models' names, essay submissions, photographs or other likenesses for the purposes of advertising, trade, publication and promotion on behalf of Harlequin Enterprises Ltd., its parent, affiliates, subsidiaries, assigns and other authorized entities involved in the judging and promotion of the contest without further compensation to any Entrant or Model, unless prohibited by law.

5. Finalists will be determined no later than October 30, 2003. Prize Winners will be determined no later than January 31, 2004. Grand Prize Winners (consisting of winning Entrant and Model) will be required to sign and return Affidavit of Eligibility/Release of Liability and Model Release forms within thirty (30) days of notification. Non-compliance with this requirement and within the specified time period will result in disqualification and an alternate will be selected. Any prize notification returned as undeliverable will result in the awarding of the prize to an alternate set of winners. All travelers (or parent/legal guardian of a minor) must execute the Affidavit of Eligibility/Release of Liability prior to ticketing and must possess required travel documents (e.g. valid photo ID) where applicable. Travel dates specified by Sponsor but no later than May 30, 2004.

6. Prizes: One (1) Grand Prize—the opportunity for the Model to appear on the cover of a paperback book from the Harlequin Blaze series, and a 3 day/2 night trip for two (Entrant and Model) to New York, NY for the photo shoot of Model which includes round-trip coach air transportation from the commercial airport nearest the winning Entrant's home to New York, NY, (or, in lieu of air transportation, $100 cash payable to Entrant and Model, if the winning Entrant's home is within 250 miles of New York, NY), hotel accommodations (double occupancy) at the Plaza Hotel and $500 cash spending money payable to Entrant and Model, (approximate prize value: $8,000), and one (1) Runner-up Prize of $200 cash payable to Entrant and Model for a romantic dinner for two (approximate prize value: $200). Prizes are valued in U.S. currency. Prizes consist of only those items listed as part of the prize. No substitution of prize(s) permitted by winners. All prizes are awarded jointly to the Entrant and Model of the winning entries, and are not severable - prizes and obligations may not be assigned or transferred. Any change to the Entrant and/or Model of the winning entries will result in disqualification and an alternate will be selected. Taxes on prize are the sole responsibility of winners. Any and all expenses and/or items not specifically described as part of the prize are the sole responsibility of winners. Harlequin Enterprises Ltd. and D.L. Blair, Inc., their parents, affiliates, and subsidiaries are not responsible for errors in printing of Contest entries and/or game pieces. No responsibility is assumed for lost, stolen, late, illegible, incomplete, inaccurate, non-delivered, postage due or misdirected mail or entries. In the event of printing or other errors which may result in unintended prize values or duplication of prizes, all affected game pieces or entries shall be null and void.

7. Winners will be notified by mail. For winners' list (available after March 31, 2004), send a self-addressed, stamped envelope to: Harlequin Blaze Cover Model Search Contest 3569 Winners, P.O. Box 4200, Blair, NE 68009-4200, or refer to the Harlequin website (at www.blazecovermodel.com).

Contest sponsored by Harlequin Enterprises Ltd., P.O. Box 9042, Buffalo, NY 14269-9042.

HBCVRMODEL2